The Whale of
the
Victoria Cross

The Whale of the

Translated from the French

by

PATRICIA WOLF

NEW YORK

Victoria Cross

BY
PIERRE BOULLE

AUTHOR OF

The Bridge Over the River Kwai

AND

Planet of the Apes

THE VANGUARD PRESS

Designer: Tom Bevans
Manufactured in the United States of America
1   2   3   4   5   6   7   8   9   0
Library of Congress Cataloging in Publication Data

Boulle, Pierre, 1912-
The whale of the Victoria Cross.

Translation of: La baleine des Malouines.
I. Title.
PQ2603.0754B313   1983   843'.914   83-14641

Attention!
On radar, cetaceans often look like subma-
rines.

— Prince Philip, Duke of Edinburgh

(From a speech made in May, 1982,
during the Falklands conflict.)

PART ONE

1

THE BRITISH fleet crossed the fiftieth parallel and soon came in sight of South Georgia. No incident had marred the voyage; boredom and seasickness were the only enemies with which some five thousand men aboard the transports still had to contend. They fought them bravely, dreaming of future exploits or performing tedious calisthenics in the limited space at hand.

The capture of South Georgia, the Lilliputian garrison of which offered token resistance, proved to be a mere formality, a minor diversion. The ships anchored there for two or three days at most, barely time for the men to reacquaint their feet with solid ground. The armada then headed at a leisurely pace for the Falkland Islands—called Malvinas by the Argentines, who had annexed them—the recapture of which was this task force's ultimate goal.

On the aircraft carrier serving as his headquarters,

the commanding admiral had invited a few guests for drinks and dinner. Two were noncombatant reserves, friends of his whose conversation he enjoyed and whose opinions he would seek whenever a broad, nonmilitary perspective seemed desirable. One was a chaplain (everyone called him the Padre; nobody knew his real name) who looked after the sailors' and soldiers' moral and spiritual welfare and comforted them in time of need. He was an excellent chaplain. The second man, a doctor, Colonel Hodges—"Doc" to most of the officers as well as the noncoms, with whom he was on the best of terms— was there to keep the troops healthy. Not just physically healthy because, in addition to practicing general medicine, he was also an eminent neurologist and not averse to turning the care of bodies over to assistants so he could concentrate on troop morale. He had been about to retire when the task force was being organized. The admiral, who had known him for years and was fond of his company, and who displayed at times a special sense of humor, talked him into coming along, insisting that a nerve specialist was sorely needed on an adventure such as the Falklands operation. The padre and the doctor were old friends, both having served in the Korean War; they got along admirably.

The third guest was the admiral's chief of staff, Captain Grant, rather shy but a model of self-possession, with an infallible memory and an incomparable knowledge of naval affairs. By relying on Grant to collect, examine, and sift through information culled from all the military services, the admiral was able to make intelligent decisions based on the predigested material presented to him. That is the function of every chief of staff. Grant possessed other valuable qualities: ever so calmly he managed to soothe the admiral's wrath whenever the Admiralty happened to deliver a particularly irksome note, or when a ship's captain had done something the admiral considered ill-advised. At such moments the normally red thicket above his eyes seemed to darken; his face turned crimson, the veins in his neck bulged, and his immediate impulse was to fire off some caustic, irreverent retort to the note, wholly in defiance of military protocol, or to chew out the offending captain for some minor transgression. Grant made sure never to confront the admiral head-on and had a knack for stalling those impulses long enough to defuse them.

Two more officers completed the admiral's guest list that evening, as the fleet was leaving South Georgia. One was the commander of the aircraft carrier; the other, the general in charge of land forces, those five thousand men assigned to recapture the Falklands. The general was quartered aboard one of the transports, among his troops, but the admiral summoned him frequently to the carrier to discuss future operations. The general made the trip by helicopter, as did the padre and Dr. Hodges when they visited other units of the fleet. It was no problem as long as the sea remained calm and the ships had not yet reached the war zone.

After exchanging a few bland remarks with his guests about the biting cold on the fringes of Antarctica and the seemingly endless crossing, the admiral got down to business. He described their situation as altogether favorable despite the fleet's slow progress, due, he explained, to the number of auxiliary vessels in the convoy and the expected arrival of reinforcements.

"There are more long days of calm and inactivity ahead of us before we encounter enemy aircraft," he declared. "No unidentified ship has been sighted. Our nuclear submarines are on watch up and down the Argentine coast. The enemy fleet is not about to confront us in open waters."

He then inquired about troop morale aboard the transports. The general reported that it was pretty good, but the long voyage was beginning to make the men fidgety and he was eager to find new ways to keep them busy.

"After all, I can't have them drilling or doing pushups from dawn to dark, when we really don't have the space for regular training exercises. As I told you, Admiral, to keep them occupied I've had my officers arrange some lectures on the history of the Falklands and the topography of the terrain on which they will have to fight. That's taken up a few hours. Apropos, Mr. Grant, thank you for providing so much information."

The chief of staff would have felt he was shirking his duty if, before sailing, he had not searched out all there was to know about the history of the islands since their discovery by John Davis in the sixteenth century, up until Britain officially occupied them in 1833, with interim incursions by France, Spain, and Argentina.

"You didn't forget the famous naval battle during

the First World War, did you?" queried the admiral.

On this subject he himself had furnished the general with many facts, and had even taken the time to prepare lecture notes to benefit the troops. He could describe every single naval engagement in detail and had worked out a lengthy memorandum on the one that took place between British and German ships in December, 1914, off the Falklands, which ended in a stunning victory for the British and their ultimate triumph in the war on the high seas.

"I didn't overlook it, Admiral."

"Well?"

"The subject appeared to hold their attention for a while," said the general after a pause, "but that's about it. They need more absorbing activities. On the other hand, some sailors who came to the talk seemed very interested."

"Strange if they weren't," grumbled the admiral.

The padre and the doctor, who spent a good deal of time among the men, confirmed the general's statements. The troops were bored.

"You understand, sir," Hodges explained, "your sailors are used to life at sea, and the ship is their second home. For the infantry, it's different. It's a rough experience for five thousand men to be cooped up on a boat for a month, in close quarters, without their usual distractions or the tough maneuvers to which they're accustomed. I've treated some pretty severe cases of depression."

"I've come across a few myself," the padre added.

"These pathologic cases are still few and far between, but the voyage had better end soon. Prolonged inaction is the worse enemy."

"Inaction and lack of human contacts," the padre reminded him.

"Rest assured, Doc, and you too, Padre," declared the admiral knowingly, "they'll soon have *action* as well as *human* contacts."

Pleased with his little sally, he chuckled to himself. At that moment the conversation broke off. An officer bearing a message just off the wires was asking to see his commander.

2

"**W**HAT is it?" Grant asked the officer, who approached upon obtaining the admiral's permission.

"Message from the Admiralty, sir."

"Important, I hope," muttered the admiral. What he really meant was that it had better be important if they had the nerve to disturb him when he was receiving guests.

"I assumed that all messages from the Admiralty were important, sir," the young officer replied calmly.

The admiral looked at him with a funny look, but the other did not bat an eyelash.

"Besides, this one is marked 'very urgent.'"

He handed a folded sheet to the chief of staff, who read it attentively and gulped with surprise. He then dismissed the officer with a shrug and the advice that there would be no immediate reply. The young man saluted, turned on his heel, and left the room.

"What's up?" the admiral asked.

"Nothing terribly important that I can see, sir. Certainly nothing worthy of the label 'very urgent.'"

"Let's have it."

The admiral took the note and began reading it nonchalantly, then stopped and began again. As he read it more deliberately the second time, a crimson flush invaded his cheeks. His eyebrows warned of the storm brewing. The padre winced as the admiral loosed a violent oath under his breath. In deference to his guests, however, he composed himself and, after a lengthy pause, which his companions patiently endured, he addressed them in icy tones of barely concealed rage.

"Gentlemen, I am sure you are anxious to know the contents of this message. You are dying to know why they choose to disturb the high command after hours. I shall satisfy your rightful curiosity. Oh, I shall not betray any military secret. A very urgent communication indeed, but not confidential. The heading says, 'FOR YOUR INFORMATION.' That's not an order, so you are the first to be informed. Listen."

He cleared his throat and began to read rapidly.

"The admiral in command of the fleet, etc . . . etc . . . is advised that as recently as last May, during a meeting of the Royal British Society for the Protection of Birds, the Duke of Edinburgh said something that caught the attention of his audience: 'Attention! On radar, cetaceans often look like submarines.' Prince Philip was speaking as president of the World Wild Life Fund. This warning will be brought to the attention of all unit commanders."

"That's it, gentlemen, every bit of it. And, I repeat,

these are not instructions—no, they wouldn't dare. Just information. I am free to act as I see fit. What do you think, Mr. Grant? Can you read between the lines as I can? Do you understand what this piece of hypocrisy, when properly deciphered, means?"

"I think it's very clear, sir," Grant replied, unruffled.

"I shall interpret it, gentlemen," the admiral went on, "for the benefit of those of you unfamiliar with the Admiralty's style. It means that if your radar signals a strange object, if your submarine detection system picks it up two hundred feet below, and if you decide to dump your entire arsenal of depth charges onto it, that's all right, that's your choice, your duty perhaps, a naval officer must be prepared to accept responsibilities. But if, after all this, the bloody, mangled body of a whale floats to the surface, we will have to hold you accountable, for when word leaks out—and it surely will, since you have a news reporter on board—the public will howl and blame the Navy right up to the ranks of its chief officers. So be warned. Isn't this correct, Mr. Grant?"

"That's about it, sir. And if, on the other hand..."

"If, on the other hand, you heed the advice of the Duke of Edinburgh (dear old Philip, bless his soul!) and are cautious, cool, and circumspect; if, before launching your depth charges, you make certain there's no whale about; if, for fear of harming some poor creature of the deep, a glorious link in nature's chain, you end up with a couple of torpedoes in your gut and you lose not just a destroyer or a cruiser but fifty sailors as well, then it's entirely your own responsibility and we will have to court-martial you for extreme negligence... How does that strike you?" he asked, turning to the carrier's captain.

He replied cheerfully, "Sir, when I was in charge of frigates and destroyers, I would not have hesitated for one second. At the first suspicious echo I would have streaked ahead and given the order to drop depth charges."

"You'd pay no attention to this information?"

"None whatever. As you pointed out, it's not an order."

"What's the infantry's reaction, general?"

"If I were a naval officer, Admiral, and found myself in such a situation, I think I'd do the same thing."

"Precisely my point. Mr. Grant, you will send this reply to the Admiralty: 'Received your information, which appears ill-advised in wartime. Filing same with freakish weather reports and astrological predictions that it would be a crime and a misfortune to treat seriously'."

"Sir, it won't be easy to send such a message," the chief of staff offered respectfully.

"Well, say it any way you like. Make it sound more polite as long as you keep the gist of it. Padre, you're star-gazing. Don't you agree with me?"

"I know too little about military matters to offer advice," replied the padre after a pause. "But I respect the right of every creature to exist, for the Lord created all living things. And this applies to the very largest whales that seem like monsters. If I remember correctly, it is written in Psalm 104: 'There go the ships: there is that leviathan whom thou hast made to play therein.'"

"Made to play!" protested the admiral, irritated. "A

game! That's exactly what this whole fuss amounts to! I have no desire to play games with the lives of my sailors."

Dr. Hodges knew the Bible nearly as well as the padre.

"As long as you're quoting Psalms, padre, you may recall a passage in Isaiah that goes like this: 'In that day, the Lord with his sore and great and strong sword, will punish leviathan the piercing serpent and he shall slay the dragon that is in the sea.'"

"How's that for you, Padre!" exclaimed the admiral, nodding approvingly.

"'The Lord with his sore and great and strong sword,'" the padre murmured softly. "You are not the Lord, Admiral, and the prophet speaks of a sword, not depth charges."

"The Bible is full of symbols one has to interpret," muttered the doctor.

"Not all cetaceans are monsters like the leviathan," pleaded the padre. "Though sperm whales can behave cruelly, most whales are peaceful, harmless creatures."

"That isn't the point!" growled the admiral.

"Anyway, don't be offended by what I've said," the padre entreated. "I'll be the first to admit that the killing of an animal, harmless or not, cannot be weighed against the loss of twenty sailors, maybe not even a single one."

"I appreciate your 'maybe.' Basically, we all agree; you are forced to come round to the military perspective."

"Basically, yes. I simply wanted to suggest that conditions could arise when the risk of losing a ship is practically nil as compared to the probability of involving a whale. In such a case, a few moments' reflection and a second check of the facts could avert a bad mistake. That, I think, is the message behind Prince Philip's warning."

"What do you say, Doc?" asked the admiral, hoping for an opinion to bolster his own.

"All things considered, sir, I believe the padre is on the right track. You yourself mentioned that an accident resulting in the death of a whale would stir worldwide protest and focus criticism on the whole fleet. I'm sure the officer in charge and all his crew would feel terribly ashamed to see a whale's carcass floating on the sea. Even you, sir..."

"I would congratulate whoever's in charge for his excellent marksmanship," the admiral snorted.

Hodges, who rarely minced words with the admiral, indicated his disbelief with a short cough. "If that were true, sir, you'd be the only man in the whole fleet to pride yourself on such a deed. In short, my opinion is that an accident of this kind would have a very bad effect on the men's morale."

The admiral shrugged peevishly but did not answer. These last remarks were beginning to bother him.

"If you permit, sir," interjected the chief of staff, "I think the decision ought to be left to the sub-chasers that may have picked up a suspicious echo."

"So you feel we ought to send on this ridiculous message to them?"

"If they are to make an informed decision, they should know about Prince Philip's warning."

"Thereby indicating that we absolve ourselves of any

responsibility in the matter, just as the Admiralty is doing with us. I don't care for this sort of thing."

"Furthermore, the end of the message specifies that the warning be communicated to the captains of all naval units. That's no mere information; it has all the earmarks of an order. If we file it instead of passing it on, we'll jeopardize our own position."

"Some orders are stupid," the admiral grunted.

"We could transmit the warning with a string of ifs, ands, and buts."

"Mr. Grant, will you please work up a message that is perfectly clear."

"I think I can do it, sir. For example, stipulate that if there is any doubt as to the nature of the sighted object..."

"If there is the *slightest* doubt," shouted the admiral, exasperated, "the duty of every commander is full speed ahead and open fire. That must be clearly stated."

"Certainly, sir."

Despite his independent streak, the admiral was a man of discipline who realized that his chief of staff was acting wisely, but he would not give in without a fight. The discussion went on for a while over empty glasses, then between himself and Grant after the others had left. One by one, each staff member was polled for his opinion. At last, sulking and mildly conscience-stricken, the admiral consented to circulate the information he had received.

The message transmitted to all ship captains required input from a dozen or more veteran heads and hands, not to mention a series of drafts that ate up most of the night, for the admiral rejected one version after another, finding the wording either too ambiguous or open to misinterpretation on the part of junior officers. Finally, at dawn, and with a sigh of resignation, he accepted the text that seemed to present the fewest risks.

This message was relayed to all skippers whose vessels beyond the fiftieth parallel were cruising in icy waters that are home to whales and other marine mammals.

3

THE CAPTAIN of the destroyer *Daring*, LCDR Clark, was pouring over the all-ships bulletin just received, the meaning of which seemed open to interpretation despite the best efforts of the admiral and his chief of staff to make it clear as crystal. As he was about to re-read it for the third time, muttering crossly under his breath, the watch officer, an inexperienced lieutenant, called out in alarm. The radar had picked up an unidentified object several miles away.

Casting a sour glance at the admiral's message, Clark shoved it into his pocket and dashed up to the bridge, where his chief officer met him on the run. The two men studied the radar screen anxiously. The watch officer had made no mistake: a black spot clearly visible against the luminous background signaled the presence of a rather large object, moving at a speed of several knots.

"Submarine, sir?" asked the young lieutenant, excited by an event that promised to break the monotony of the long voyage. "Or a ship? Maybe an enemy ship."

"No enemy surface craft would venture alone in these waters," muttered the chief officer. "It looks to be a submarine."

"Submarine or whale," the lieutenant commander agreed, nodding his head, adding, for his own benefit, the phrase he had just memorized:

"Attention! On radar, cetaceans often look like submarines."

A sudden wave of revolt overtook him against the injustice of having had this warning shoved under his nose minutes before, as if to cast doubt in his mind. "Just my luck!" he muttered through clenched teeth; "This kind of coincidence only happens to me!"

The destroyer *Daring* was an escort vessel fitted for antisubmarine warfare. It sailed well ahead of the main task force, flanked by two frigates port and starboard, which followed behind at some distance.

"It's dead ahead and we're gaining on it, sir," the chief officer reported. "If it's a sub, it's already in range."

"Right. But it could also be a harmless fishing boat that's wandered off course."

Clark gave orders to try to communicate with any vessel that was out there. All efforts were useless; no answer came from the mysterious object. The alarm sounded. Men dashed to their battle stations and prepared to commence firing on command. But the lieutenant commander hesitated.

"Tell Bjorg to join me on the bridge," he said to his chief officer. "He knows more about whales than anyone."

For the thought that there might indeed be a whale out there began to plague him and left him uncertain what to do.

Bjorg was not part of the destroyer's regular crew. He was a former whaler who, from hunting and killing the animals, had developed a great affection for them. Born on the larger of the two Falkland Islands, he had spent many years tracking whales between the Orkneys and South Georgia. Before turning fifty, he retired to England where his interest in marine mammals induced him to become a dolphin trainer. The dolphins, like surrogate whales, eased his longing for the adventurous life he had left behind, besides providing him with a comfortable income from exhibitions of his marine pupils.

Like many Falklanders, Bjorg had Scandinavian roots (his Nordic features and a mop of blond hair made him look like a Viking). His family had lived on a farm near Port Stanley, the capital, where he spent his childhood before going to sea. His father, also a former whaler, was not the one to inspire Bjorg with a passion for catching— or rather hunting—marine monsters. Early in his career, the father had given up whaling for sheep-raising, and thus earned the undying contempt of his own father, Bjorg's grandfather, whose tales of adventure had inflamed his grandson's imagination. The old man was a product of Herman Melville's heroic era. He was immensely proud of having been a veteran harpooner— unlike the modern gunners who, from the safety of a solid ship, can blow a sea giant to smithereens by means of a projectile fitted with an explosive charge, leaving the crew merely to claim the floating carcass and tow it to a factory ship. No, his memories were infinitely more vivid. In his day, a handful of brave men in a frail little boat would approach almost within arm's length of a whale or cachalot, whose colossal bulk made their tiny skiff look like a nutshell. Just a few yards from the giant they lanced a hand harpoon: taut muscles went limp, and the boat took to plunging about wildly under the thrashing blows of the mammoth tail. As a child, Bjorg never tired of hearing how the whaleboat rode the waves, the line winding out from the winch, the beast surging ahead or plunging deep until it surfaced to breathe, blowing up a cloud of vapor visible for miles. Lastly, the lance attack, the death-dealing blow and final frenzied convulsions that left the seas blanketed with blood.

Bjorg had relived this epic a hundred times, not only in his grandfather's memories, but also in every book on whales he could find, from *Moby Dick* to fantastic novels that stir and excite childish imaginations.

At sixteen he left the island with a job aboard a whaler. Only when the ship anchored there did he return to the Falklands. He himself had never known the era of the heroic harpooners. In his day, fishing was regulated, carried on by organized fleets of Norwegian, British, and Japanese vessels cruising the southern seas.

Nevertheless he consoled himself by inhaling the scents of the ocean, mixed with the smell of oil from the dismembering of some giant catch; by marveling at the movements of schools of sperm whales that existed in those days; and especially by sharing the thrill of the lookout man perched high in the masthead on sighting the vapor jet spouting into the air from a whale's exhaled breath. This exciting event always translated into the familiar cry famous in the whaling world, which Bjorg's grandfather would sing out in a cracked voice, but no less rapturously than in his younger days:

"Tha'ar she blows!"

Bjorg himself had been a lookout many times (he had done just about every job there was to do on a whaler, from deck-swabbing to harpoon gunning, alas!). Sometimes he was the first to spot the vapor jet and shout "Tha'ar she blows!", the visions of mad Captain Ahab's relentless pursuit of Moby Dick in his head.

The night after one such brilliant exploit (for it was a great honor to be the first to send up the cry), he would invariably wake with a start from fitful dreams, rousing his sleeping companions with the same piercing yell. He still dreamed those vivid scenes occasionally and cried out in the middle of the night, though he had long since given up hunting and killing for the peaceful occupation of dolphin trainer. His affection for marine mammals probably assumed different expressions at different times in his life. In any event, dreams helped preserve the magic of the past in the face of his relatively unmagical current activity—dreams and a flow of books about whaling and all sorts of adventure.

During the weeks of preparation before the expedition got under way, the high command had sent out a call for men or women familiar with the Falklands who could serve as guides for the landing forces. Few answered the call. Falklanders were mainly sheep farmers who seldom migrated; they lived and died on their farms. A man like Bjorg was a rare gem, for having grown up in Port Stanley and having been a sailor, he knew every creek and canal. He grabbed at the chance to join the convoy, delighted at the prospect of seeing homeland and old friends again and cruising once more in southern waters. Leaving the dolphins in charge of a capable son, he went aboard the *Daring*. Even if it wasn't a whaling ship, at least it was a boat.

Rigged out in a uniform with lieutenant's stripes scarcely befitting his years, and given the nebulous title of administrative officer, he had gone to work on an elaborate description of the future battlefield, illustrated with sketches from memory. In his leisure moments he was happy doing something he had always loved: inhaling the smells carried on the ocean spray. No one ever heard him complain about the long voyage. LCDR Clark liked him from the start and treated him as a guest, finding occasions to chat with him and to hear whaling tales about ships and crews unlike any he had had the privilege of commanding.

So when Clark felt greatly perplexed, worried about the whales because of Prince Philip's warning, yet tempted to open fire and then overwhelmed with guilt, it wasn't surprising that he could not make up his mind. Nor was it surprising that he sought out the whale expert, hoping to gain some insight into the dilemma facing him.

4

WHILE Bjorg was hurrying to the bridge, Clark had informed the high command of the radar signal but had not received any instructions. The admiral was tempted to issue a command, but his chief of staff talked him out of it, claiming that in this instance it was best to let the ship captains make their own decisions. The admiral came to the conclusion that this was the wisest course of action and said so in a brief telephone conversation, his icy tone purposely masking his own uncertainty.

"Do whatever you yourself think best and keep me informed. I am slowing the convoy and alerting all units of the fleet."

Though he would have preferred an order, Clark expected this. It was up to him and only him, captain of the *Daring,* to shoulder the responsibilities. He hesitated still, sighed, and glared at the moving dark spot on the radar screen. Bjorg found him there with the watch officer, while the chief officer rushed about the destroyer checking that every man was at his battle station.

"It could be a whale, sir," said Bjorg. While in uniform, he insisted on "sirring" the lieutenant commander, who had asked him often enough to drop the formalities.

"Probably a large whale. Not unusual in these waters. On one of my last whaling jobs I ran into the same signal."

The whaling ship in question had been equipped with radar and other electronic devices for detecting whales as well as icebergs.

"The speed is just about right for a whale," he went on.

The radar operator was calculating the mysterious object's speed and reporting it regularly, while a tracing plotted its path.

"Just about right for a whale," muttered Clark in disgust. "I expected something more positive from you. It's also just about right for a submarine. Prince Philip should have added: 'Attention also! On radar, submarines often look like whales'."

The two men gazed at the screen in silence.

"Look, Bjorg," exclaimed Clark, "it's coming toward us."

In fact, the object, formerly traveling at an angle to the destroyer, had altered its path and was now heading straight for the ship.

"It's seen us and is preparing to attack," the lieutenant commander declared. "There's no time to lose."

"Very strange, I must say," muttered the former whaler, "and disturbing. Cetaceans normally aren't afraid, but I've never known one to swim straight at a ship."

Clark was about to command his men to open fire when the spot suddenly vanished from the screen.

"The image is gone," was the confirmation received by telephone from the technician following the scene on another screen in the detection room. "The radar's lost the thing; it probably went into a dive."

"Thanks! I was aware of that," muttered the lieutenant commander.

And in a rush of guilt he cursed himself for having temporized. "Too late to obtain a fix before it fires torpedoes," he groaned. "You and your whale stories, Bjorg. I'm not fit to command a warship. It's diving—or it has dived and is coming straight for us."

"It's perfectly possible that it's *sounding*, sir. That's the word they use on every fishing boat when one of those beasts decides to visit the ocean depths. Some, like the cachalot, can descend over a mile."

"And I'm telling you that a submarine is *diving*. It's in a dive right now, do you hear? That's the word used in every navy all over the world."

"Aye, aye, sir," Bjorg replied with polite determination, "but if it's a whale, as I'm now tempted to believe, it's sounding. No two ways about it."

"Mr. Bjorg," Clark began. . . . The "mister," a form of address he rarely used for his guest, betrayed Clark's agitation.

"Mr. Bjorg, I didn't bring you out here to have you give me a lesson in linguistics."

Suddenly realizing how ridiculous the argument was

under the circumstances, he dropped the matter and began afresh.

"I think you said, 'I'm tempted to believe.' What makes you believe it's a whale when a minute ago you thought the object's behavior was alarming?"

"It sudden disappearance from the screen, sir. Did you notice that the image vanished all at once, like a snuffed-out candle? I'm no expert on submarines, but I don't suppose they dive so rapidly. Whales do."

"At last you're telling me something reasonable, Bjorg," Clark responded after a pause, feeling better now. "It's true no submarine disappears so fast, at least none of the current models, although a midget sub perhaps could do it in a pinch. But I admit this factor supports your whale theory."

"It's just my opinion, sir."

The lieutenant commander thought further and still felt undecided. "But it's not a sure thing. After spotting us, maybe it's preparing right now to attack.... Bjorg," he continued, weighing each word carefully, "suppose— this is just supposing, now—that it's a whale that has... sounded, as you call it. You see, I'm making concessions to your vocabulary as well as to your point of view. If we suppose this, how long will it remain invisible?"

"That depends, sir."

While they were talking and Clark was trying to relieve his own impatience and anxiety, a plane had left the carrier and was circling the spot where the destroyer had reported sighting the object.

"Too late, he'll never see a thing," Clark commented with a shrug. "Whatever it is is on the bottom. You say it depends, Bjorg?"

"Yes, sir. Of course, it will have to surface. Whales, as I'm sure you know, are not fish but air-breathing mammals like ourselves, and..."

"I asked you how long, Mr. Bjorg."

"Well, some have been known to stay submerged for forty to forty-five minutes."

"Forty to forty-five minutes!" exclaimed the lieutenant commander. "You mean we have to put up with another half hour of this torture?"

"That's the maximum time. On the average, whales sound for shorter periods, say fifteen to twenty minutes. It depends on the mood they're in."

"That really does it!" the officer groaned. "I don't know if my nerves can stand much more of this."

The nerves of the *Daring*'s crew were just as strained as the skipper's. This always happened and was perfectly normal when an enemy submarine approached, but the possibility of confronting a whale, which the whole crew now knew about, added a grain of spice to the adventure. Officers, chiefs, and sailors held their breath; the gun crews poised over their guns or depth charges went on mentally rehearsing each motion they would make once the command was given. But no command came.

"If it continued to dive in the same direction," murmured Clark, "it ought to be under our keel by now."

"Sir," the watch officer shouted, "it's not far away; the detector has just picked it up."

With radar now useless, the sonar technicians interrogated the asdic (Anti-Submarine Detection Investigation Committee), or sonar, which provided the means to sound-scan the ocean floor and locate an enemy craft by the echo from an ultrasonic beam.

Clark and Bjorg walked over to another screen. Just as the watch officer had reported, the mysterious object, whether a deadly submarine or an innocent cetacean, was quite visible in the form of a new spot standing out against the sea, pictured by the sonar as a continuous curve on a strip of paper. A message from the detection room confirmed this occurrence.

"Lucky it's been picked up again," murmured Clark, heaving a sigh of relief.

"I don't agree, sir."

Bjorg was studying the spot anxiously, as if awaiting some reaction. When none came, he looked disgusted.

"Don't agree with you at all, sir," he repeated gravely. "It's certainly not an encouraging sign. I don't like it one bit."

"Why not?"

"I have no personal experience with sonar, but I know the instrument has been used to try to detect whales in deep waters. Well, after a number of attempts, according to what I've heard, it was finally realized that ultrasonic sounds, inaudible to the human ear, are highly audible to whales."

"So what?"

"Well, sir, as soon as the vibrations reach them, they run for it. I don't think that's what's happening here. This thing, if it is a whale, which I'm beginning to doubt, keeps plodding along as if it had nothing else to do. When you get down to it," he went on in the quiet voice that exasperated Clark, "your fears may be justified. It's very possible we're facing a submarine."

"What did I tell you!" shouted Clark. "You come around here tranquilizing me with your whale stories when we're up against a bloody sub! And it's headed straight for our keel! I know what I have to do if it isn't too late."

He grabbed for the telephone, ready to order full speed ahead and prepare to drop depth charges. A cry from the former whaler, whose eyes were glued to the sonar screen, made him hesitate once more.

5

CLARK froze, his hand on the telephone.

"What is it now, Mr. Bjorg?" he pleaded in a strained voice.

"It's done an about-face and is fleeing, sir. Must be picking up the ultrasonic beam. Case of delayed reaction, that's all. Look for yourself."

Unconsciously, the lieutenant commander dabbed at his forehead where a few drops of sweat had formed in defiance of the biting cold. Bjorg's manner was so persuasive that Clark held off issuing battle commands and went to examine the sonar screen. The object effectively had made a 180-degree turn and was heading away from the destroyer in the same direction it had come.

"It doesn't look frantic. What I mean is, this object doesn't seem bothered by our sonar," Clark said anxiously. "Didn't you tell me that the asdic beam affects whales like an electric shock: on contact with it, they flee in panic? But this one isn't moving fast."

"What I said applied to certain whales, sir, but, to my knowledge, few experiments have been done with sonar, surely not enough to establish a general rule. Anyway, there are whales and whales. It's possible that the finback doesn't react like the sperm whale, for example, or the right whale, or even the blue whale. There are any number of species, sir, from..."

"Mr. Bjorg," the officer interjected impatiently, "kindly spare me a display of your whaling knowledge. I can assure you this is not the moment."

"I just wanted to explain, sir, that you can't jump to conclusions when so little research has been done."

"Then we won't jump to conclusions. And we'll have to put up with more of this confounded uncertainty. Meanwhile, whatever it is dived more than ten minutes ago."

"The point, sir, is that it reacted to the ultrasonic beam in one way or another: it turned around. No submarine would have done that."

"Could have been sheer coincidence."

"Possibly. But there's something else, a very significant fact, I think, that ought to make you feel better, because now I'm convinced it's a whale."

"What? What significant fact?" Clark pursued eagerly, impressed as always by this expert's self-assurance.

"Even two facts, sir. The first... You weren't looking at the screen when the turnabout occurred. Well, I was watching carefully, and it turned on a dime. I don't believe any submarine, even a midget, could swing around in such a small radius. But a whale can."

"Now you're talking sense," Clark declared approvingly after a moment's thought. "In fact, a submarine can't turn around in place."

He checked with the detection room and was informed that the object had indeed reversed its direction just as Bjorg said. Furthermore, the hydrophones—devices that register engine vibrations—had not picked up any special signal.

"But this still isn't absolute proof," Clark lamented. "These instruments are not accurate at the depth of this object and don't always differentiate between the sounds of a submarine and of our own ship. And anyway, some underwater motors are virtually silent."

Glancing at his watch again, he sighed and kept silent, gazing at the radar screen. At their stations on the destroyer, the sailors shared the skipper's impatience, though not his anguish, for the responsibility was his alone.

"Didn't you mention a second observation that suggests the presence of a whale?" Clark asked at last.

"Equally significant, sir. I told you that I watched the screen most carefully. Well, just at the moment of turning, in a fraction of a second, I had the impression the image split in two."

"Split in two? What the devil are you getting at?"

"It doesn't show up when the object swims in a straight line; then the spot looks slightly fuzzy. Your sonar probably isn't too accurate. But during the turn, I repeat, though I can't swear to it, I think I saw two spots instead of one, with a tiny interval between. That could mean..."

"I know what you're driving at," the lieutenant commander shouted angrily. "You'd have me believe..."

"You guessed it, sir. That's exactly what I'm driving at. My eyes are fine and I wasn't seeing things. It means we're dealing with two whales."

"Two whales!" Clark moaned softly.

"Yes, sir, two," Bjorg insisted cheerfully. "A couple, male and female; two whales swimming side by side with barely a sliver of space between. When they swim in a straight line, flipper to flipper (that's what the lateral fins are called), your sonar as well as your radar instruments show a single image—the separating element isn't strong enough. When making a half circle, however, the whales have to move apart, and that's what I saw. Two whales, I'm almost certain. Probably blue whales, I should add, the largest in the world. Blue whales are monogamous and normally travel in pairs, unlike sperm whales, which usually gather in large groups."

"Bless you, Bjorg!" Clark exclaimed. "One whale already was more than I could handle; next you'll be sending me a herd."

"Pod, sir."

"What?"

"Whalingmen call a large congregation of cetaceans a 'pod.' I doubt if we'll run into any, except perhaps orcas. Pods of cachalots were still around in my younger days, and I've sighted a few in different waters. The hunters have forced them to disperse, but it's still fairly common to meet a pair of whales."

The lieutenant commander shrugged and went out to telephone the chief of detection to question him about the information provided by Bjorg. He returned looking dejected. What he had learned left him even more bewildered.

"One or two observers think they saw a double image as you did, but not the others. And the ones who saw it aren't even sure they did; they feel it could have been a momentary disruption of the sonar. The officer in charge tells me that happens constantly."

"Indeed, sir," Bjorg pursued subbornly, "but as I said, I have excellent vision and what I saw has nothing to do with submarines. Two such craft would never cruise side by side less than ten feet apart."

"All of which adds up to the fact that we must endure more of this intolerable uncertainty," Clark groaned.

He glanced at his watch again, rolled his eyes morosely, and fell into a brooding silence. On the asdic screen the spot kept moving at the same leisurely pace; the object was traveling in the same direction as the destroyer, at nearly the same speed.

"Your uncertainty is about to end, sir," Bjorg declared. "They're coming up for air."

The whaler was right. Against the ocean background, the spot was mounting to the surface.

"Almost vertically," he went on. "Would a submarine rise in that fashion? In a couple of minutes they'll emerge and the radar can pick them up again. Perhaps we'll even be able to see them ourselves; they're not too far away."

"Let's pray for that. I won't feel normal again until

I've seen them with my own eyes. But I doubt if the weather will permit it."

The wind had come up and a surging swell limited the view.

"I'd love to know what's going to appear," Clark murmured.

Leaving the screen, he went to telephone instructions to his chief officer. His voice and gestures were unusually harsh and punctuated, as if he expected to find a general slacking off in the performance of duties since no enemy had appeared during the previous half hour.

"You must bear in mind that we will have to be doubly watchful and ready for whatever happens," he lectured the officer. "Just because some people think there are whales around is no excuse to let down our guard. In fact, we have no idea what is going to surface. All stations must be prepared to fire artillery and torpedoes on command."

"Do you still think it could be an enemy sub, sir?"

"I don't think anything. I want to be ready for everything and everyone."

"Aye, aye, sir."

Privately, the chief officer felt the skipper was overreacting. He was. The tensions of the last half hour had so jangled the nerves of this normally stable lieutenant commander that he imagined all sorts of things. He was trimming his sails, preparing to confront some sea monster rising from the ocean floor, more formidable than a fleet of submarines or a legendary phantom ship with the devil at the helm and all his crew.

Reassured somewhat by the chief officer's insistence

that all hands remain vigilant and prepared to man the guns at a moment's notice, he returned to the screens.

"Where did Bjorg go?" he asked.

The young officer was still there. His watch had ended and his replacement now stood on the bridge, but nothing in the world could have pried him away from this thrilling scene. With a pair of field glasses he was scouring the sea. The two screens were blank: the sonar had lost its prey, the radar had not yet captured it. It was he who responded to Clark's query.

"Bjorg?" he repeated, turning around. "I don't know, sir. He was here a minute ago."

The lieutenant commander had no time to complain about the whale expert's absence. A yell, more like a whoop, exploded overhead, as if bursting out of the leaden skies, rising above the wailing wind, and freezing every member of the *Daring*'s crew in his tracks.

"She blows! She blows! Didn't I tell you, sir! Tha'ar she blows!"

6

"**W**HERE the devil are you, Bjorg?" complained the captain of the *Daring*.

"Up here, sir, over your head, against the radar antenna. It's the highest point on the ship, and I can see farther than from the bridge. She's spouting! Her mate has surfaced too. They're both spouting! Look, over there, sir!"

The roof of the bridge blocked Clark's view of the antenna, but some of the sailors on deck peered up to see the former whaler clutching the mast that supported the radar, his mop of blond hair streaming in the wind, one arm waving frantically in the direction of a spot on the far horizon that he had been the first to observe, vocally and actively reliving the thrilling saga of his earlier days. How he had managed to climb up there was not Clark's immediate concern. Surprised at first, soon he was basking in a glow of glorious relief at the load that had slipped off his shoulders.

"They're spouting!" he repeated. "Praise the Lord! Are you sure this time?"

"No doubt about it. Dead ahead, sir, less than three miles. They're slowing down and we're getting nearer. Soon you'll be able to see them. A pair, just as I thought. Two magnificent specimens of the blue whale. I don't think I ever harpooned such huge ones."

Bjorg's excitement spread contagiously among the sailors, who stared wide-eyed at this devil of a fellow gesticulating wildly and clinging to the mast like a spider to its web. His shouts electrified the crew. Up on the bridge, Clark thought he heard the call echoing from every part of the ship:

"Tha'ar she blows! Tha'ar she blows!"

"Tha'ar she blows, sir!" yelled the young lieutenant in turn as he scoured the horizon in the direction indicated by a hastily mounted watch.

"I see them! I see them!" cried the lieutenant commander, swept along by the infectious emotion. "They're spouting! God bless you, Bjorg! You were right."

Then, in a desperate effort to recover his dignity, he commanded, "Mr. Bjorg, will you kindly come down from a perch on which nobody authorized you to perch. You are likely to tumble onto the deck and break your neck, or fall overboard. Even if neither prospect bothers you, at least do me the favor of sparing our radar antenna further damage."

"Coming right down, sir."

A quick series of contortions worthy of a professional

acrobat, proving that Bjorg, despite his fifty years, had lost none of his sailor's agility, landed him, after one final somersault, on the bridge next to Clark. The gymnast apologized briefly.

"I thought you wanted an answer as soon as possible. I had the best chance of getting it up there."

"Let's forget it," Clark mumbled. "You've relieved me of a great burden. I'm in no mood to chew you out, but please don't do it again."

The depression weighing on the *Daring*'s skipper had floated away, leaving him with a curious lightheadedness—and sore muscles, as if from a sound thrashing. For a long time he remained silent, bent over a handrail on the bridge, watching the two whales with a look of mixed resentment and gratitude. The wind seemed to be falling and the sky clearing; the waves were settling down. The undulating forms of the whales stood out clearly now, each topped with a vaporous spray, or a magical irridescence when a ray of sunlight chanced to pierce the clouds. Clark at last was able to appreciate the poetry of the scene.

"They can clap themselves on the back for having put me through a grueling half hour," he sighed, "and should thank the god of whales for dear old Philip's warning."

The two whales were swimming so close to the destroyer that their distinctive features emerged.

"Blue whales you said, didn't you?" Clark asked. "How could you tell just from seeing their spout? Why not sperm whales, which share these waters too, I think?"

The former whaler shot him a pitying glance. "Surely

not sperm whales, sir. Note the shape of the spray projecting from their blowholes: it shoots straight up like the stem of a flower, opening out at the top, then falls seaward like the fronds of a palm tree or the arms of a weeping willow. The sperm whale's breath emerges obliquely rather than vertically because of the location of its blowholes. As for the fact these are blue whales, there's no mistaking it. First of all, their size. The one on the right, the larger one, must be the female, and at least a hundred feet long. The male is slightly shorter. No other marine mammal is so huge. And if you want further proof, note the belly of these beasts when they start to turn sideways as they're doing now: grayish-blue dappled with white and grooved with horizontal pleats. That's the apparel of the blue whale."

The former whaler's experienced eye singled out other details that no ordinary observer would ever notice. Clark liked to hear him talk and felt that auditing this lecture on animal lore was his well-deserved reward for all the anxiety the animals had caused him. A telephone call rudely snatched him from his reverie.

"The Admiral, sir," announced the watch officer, who had answered the phone.

"Good Lord!" Clark exclaimed. "He wanted me to call him every five minutes and advise him of any new development. I forgot, when the whales appeared."

"Yes, sir, awaiting your orders."

"I'm awaiting your report," came the admiral's ice-laden voice. "I thought I made it clear that I wanted to be informed."

"They are spouting, sir!" Clark declared triumphantly, like a captain announcing a stunning victory. "Tha'ar she blows, sir!"

After all the excitement, he could find no better words to sum up the situation than the legendary cry of the whale hunters, which still rang in his ears, leaped out of the sky, and echoed from the bowels of his ship.

"What's that you're telling me?" growled the admiral.

"They're spouting, sir. There are two of them," Clark went on hurriedly, "a male and a female. I see them right in front of us, less than half a mile away."

"You mean to tell me it was a whale, not an enemy submarine? I presume, Mr. Clark, that is how I am to interpret your speech, which is not very lucid."

"Two whales, sir. They surfaced a few minutes ago."

"A few minutes? You might have informed me. Don't you think I am anxious to know the outcome of this alert, just as anxious as you must have been?"

"I was about to do it, sir."

"H-m-m . . . Are you sure they are whales?"

"Positive, sir. Bjorg, the whalingman I brought along, identified them the minute they surfaced. Huge blue whales at least a hundred feet long, spouting gigantic vapor jets straight into the air! You can even see the ventral pleats characteristic of the species."

He would have liked to display more of his newly acquired knowledge, but the admiral cut him short, having no interest in such matters.

"That will do, Mr. Clark. Relax. I imagine your present excitement stems from the stress and strain you have been through—we all have been through. Anyway, everything has turned out for the best: you haven't been torpedoed and you've saved two whales. Prince Philip would be deliriously happy to hear about this. I guess I ought to congratulate you for keeping a cool head," he added grudgingly, after a pause. "Any other captain would have fired first and asked questions later. All the same, I have one comment to make."

He spoke slowly and deliberately, selecting his words, as if some grave concern preyed on his mind.

"I wish you would explain to me as precisely as possible what made you think you were dealing with whales. I presume your reasons were significant."

Clark described what had made him act as he did, adding that Bjorg's opinion had been a deciding factor. The admiral listened attentively and did not interrupt.

"So you had what can be called a reasonable certainty," he remarked at last.

"Certainty? Not exactly, sir, sorry to say. I seesawed between confidence and doubt. Now that I think of it, I suppose you could call it probability."

A slight cough from the admiral indicated that this response was unsatisfactory.

"How probable? Ninety-nine percent? Ninety percent? Less?"

"I couldn't tell you exactly, sir," Clark admitted, his head beginning to flutter. "I never asked myself the question. It was a very, very strong probability, that's all I can say."

"Good," grumbled the admiral, less convinced than ever. "Anyway, it's the result that counts, and the result seems to prove you acted properly. Let's drop the subject. I'm not trying to criticize you; I really feel you deserve congratulations."

"Thank you, sir."

"One more word. I want you to know that if you had decided to act differently, if you had knocked off those two blasted whales, I wouldn't have blamed you. And I might add that if a similar incident occurs..."

Now the admiral's voice grew warm and paternal, as if he were offering his own son a word of fatherly advice about life's perils.

"If a similar alert should recur, try not to be swayed by the thought that your watchful waiting paid off this time, and act as if you face a different set of circumstances. Understand?"

"Aye, aye, sir."

"I trust I've made myself clear," the admiral muttered to himself, having ended the conversation. "Blasted whales!"

Clark returned to find Bjorg still observing the animals. He was about to order an end to the state of alert when a shout from the watch officer raised a fresh alarm.

"Another radar signal, sir. No, not our two whales; the new object is far away from them."

7

STAGGERED by this latest blow, the lieutenant commander froze in his tracks, cursing his bad luck to have been elected fate's preferred target for the day. If this next ordeal were to drag on like the last one, would he have the courage, he wondered, to face it boldly and coolly as any captain of a destroyer should? He decided to rejoin Bjorg, whose puckered brow was less than reassuring. Frowning grimly, the former whaler declared in a voice of doom:

"No use watching the radar screen, sir. I can see it as clearly as I see you."

The ocean was fairly calm now, and the view extended for miles. As he watched them, Clark noticed something odd about the whales' behavior. They had turned suddenly and raced off, as if in headlong flight. Looking where Bjorg pointed, he thought he could see something moving on the ocean's face, and his old anxiety returned as he recalled the admiral's admonition.

"Periscope?"

"No, sir," replied the young lieutenant, who was still on the bridge with his field glasses trained on the water. "I see something too, but I'm sure it can't be a periscope. It's a kind of black triangular sail skimming the surface at tremendous speed, much faster than the wind's blowing."

Clark snatched the binoculars, but before he could locate the new apparition, Bjorg injected a second, equally ominous comment.

"No indeed, it's no periscope, sir. This time we can be certain. Don't give it another thought. There's no enemy out there—not *your* enemy at least. The whales wouldn't agree, though. See them fleeing in panic. The poor creatures know the fate in store for them."

"What's this all about? Explain yourself, will you?" Clark exclaimed impatiently, too nervous to adjust the binoculars.

"A killer, sir."

"Killer?"

"The killer, or killer whale as they're sometimes known. There must be many others in the area; killers always attack in packs. Poor whales!... The *grampus orca*, if you prefer the Latin name, or just plain orca. That black triangle slicing the waves like a knife blade is its dorsal fin. Some fins reach a height of five feet; this one must be pretty big. And, I remind you, they never appear singly; being cowards, they gang up on their victims."

As if to confirm this, the watch officer announced, "Two, four, five spots on the screen. A dozen now. I've lost count. ..."

"I see them too," Bjorg declared. "About twenty; soon there'll be a hundred. Others are drifting in from all over the ocean, drawn by their favorite prey and the promise of a fine feast. These are the whale's predatory foe, as well as the seal's if there's nothing tastier to feed on. Our poor whales don't stand a chance against them. I've never watched killers at work, but from what I've heard, it's a gory scene. ... What did I tell you? First the roundup, now the assault and the inevitable slaughter."

Panic-stricken, after trying vainly to elude their attackers by swimming a zigzag course, the two whales had approached the destroyer. Watchers on the bridge could actually see the dorsal fins of the orcas as they circled their prey in ever-narrowing rings.

"In *The Great Adventure of the Whales*," Bjorg continued, "Georges Blond described such a battle—if that's what you call this ruthless butchery. At a signal, the attack is on. Like a pack of wild dogs they hurl themselves at the smaller of the two whales, most probably the male. These devils use a vicious tactic: what we're seeing bears out the reports of certain navigators, which in turn were confirmed by R.C. Andrews, a highly respected cetacean expert who was also a learned naturalist and fearless mariner. Watch: a pack pounces on the tail, which serves as the whale's propeller. If they manage to crush it— they have deadlier jaws than the most ferocious sharks— the whale is immobilized and helpless. Another pack rushes sideways at the head, to force open the victim's mouth and seize its most sensitive organ, the tongue, which they will devour even before killing the prey. The whale fights desperately; it twists and turns and writhes and leaps to prodigious heights, trying to crush the hunters under its massive bulk—the only weapon it has."

"It's putting up a brave defense," declared the young lieutenant, who seemed both impressed and angered by the one-sided struggle.

"I think one of them is dead," reported the watch officer in the same tone of voice.

"Maybe, but a kill only makes the others more bloodthirsty. Look, over there! What did I tell you? They've grabbed the tip of its tongue."

"Appalling," murmured the young lieutenant. "You're right, it's a slaughter."

Crewmen who were free to follow the struggle agreed. Indignant protests and murmurs of horror rose from all parts of the ship. Relieved to know he had to contend only with whales, Clark was now feeling the same revulsion as the others. Rather than show it, however, he tried to shift attention to matters bearing on the Falklands operation. He reprimanded the young lieutenant.

"Mr. Hudson, if this sight breaks your heart and makes you want to weep, nobody is asking you to look. I must remind you that we are at war. So far we've only had to deal with whales, and I think we should rejoice at having encountered a pack of orcas instead of a submarine fleet. These animals are not the enemy."

Thus admonished, Hudson hung his head and said

nothing. Bjorg was silent too, but the glance he shot at the *Daring*'s skipper bore a hint of reproach. Clark also had the uncomfortable impression that everyone else, including his chief officer, who had just returned to the bridge, thought he was acting unfairly. He was sorry he had opened his mouth. With a shrug of annoyance he turned back to watch the death scene.

For the first whale the end was near. The tactics used by the rapacious killers were paying off. With its tail firmly in the grip of several sets of jaws, the immobilized animal pitched about wildly at first, then its writhing grew feebler. The lead pack had begun to devour the tongue, as Bjorg predicted. The giant rose for the last time and collapsed back into the arms of the playful crimson waves.

The rush for the spoils was on. The killers swarmed over the carcass instantly, ripping and slashing with a ferocity that soon reduced it to a massive chunk of shapeless flesh. The fracas caused by the violent struggle seemed to have traveled far and wide, owing to the acute senses of marine creatures, and was attracting other orcas equally fond of blubber and blood. One after another new black sails appeared on the horizon, and when there was no more room at the feast taking place before the indignant sailors, the killers turned on the second whale.

"The female is in for it now," groaned Bjorg in despair. "These devils are rarely satisfied; they never abandon a prey at hand."

Once again his predictions proved true. The black triangular fins of the latest arrivals converged on the second whale. The same repugnant scene was about to repeat itself. Two orcas had moved in to lead the attack. Two sets of jaws had clamped down on the victim's tail in order to immobilize it. Clark heard cries of digust and horror from the crew. But the whale defended herself fiercely, even more energetically than had her mate. Or had the two killers advanced too boldly beyond the pack? The whale gave a tremendous leap, projecting more than half her length out of the water, shaking off her assailants and freeing herself from their hold. Crashing back on them with her full force in a gigantic tower of foam, she managed to disable both predators. One was struck dead and bobbed belly-up on the waves; the other, stunned, had retreated to await reinforcements.

Applause thundered and shouts rang from every corner of the ship. At that moment Clark felt something he had never felt during all the time he commanded the *Daring:* a curious impression that his destroyer was a living creature in possession of the full range of human emotions, including indignation, fury, and excitement.

Young Lieutenant Hudson, clinging to the bridge railing with trembling hands, raised an impassioned cheer. Safe for the moment, the whale rushed off, leaving a faint trail of blood in her wake. She had won a battle, but the war's outcome was fairly certain. In panic, she raced headlong toward the orcas feeding on her mate, many of which turned to bar her path.

"She's surrounded," Bjorg moaned. "I told you the killers never abandon a prey."

Suddenly, just before her assailants lunged at her, the whale made a last desperate leap and, rotating her arched body, plunged forward. For a fraction of a second, while three-quarters of her bulk was immersed, the gigantic tail stood up nearly straight in the water, then disappeared. All that remained were the orcas, their fins lazily circling the turbulent foam.

"She's diving!" cried Clark.

"Sounding," the whaler corrected him. "It's a last-ditch effort, but it won't give her much time or save her in the end. The killers can't follow her to the bottom where she's hiding; they're not even trying to. Look at them: they're not going anywhere, just waiting patiently for her to reappear while they swim round and round, keeping watch. They know she won't escape."

"If she stays under for forty minutes, as you said she could, she'll be able to cover quite a distance and has a good chance of getting away," Clark offered.

"Not the ghost of a chance, sir. Panic, flight, and a violent struggle have nearly winded her; she can't stay submerged more than a few minutes. The killers know that; they're clever. In the Antarctic, when the seals they hunt take refuge on a chunk of ice floe, what do you think the orcas do? They dive and dash themselves against the ice to capsize it and dislodge the prey, which other pack members seize and devour. Captain Scott reported that such an incident had befallen one of his photographers installed on a strip of ice adjoining an ice bank. The unwary fellow was lucky enough to tumble onto the ice bank instead of into the water. Still, orcas are not considered man-eaters: too intelligent for that. They fear reprisal. According to the story, they were only after the photographer's dog and probably mistook it for a seal or some other marine animal."

"There she is!" shouted Lieutenant Hudson. "Holy Mother! She didn't swim very far, but now she's closer to us. Look, she can't be more than a quarter of a mile away."

8

IN FACT the blue whale had surfaced fairly close to the destroyer in a tumultuous geyser of foam, while the hunters waited in the distance. Now she was swimming alongside the ship, still trailing blood in her wake, a vestige of the first attack. The wound apparently was not too serious, for she had no trouble keeping up with the ship. But she was growing weak; she panted, and her labored breathing as she exhaled vast quantities of spent air from her lungs sounded to the crew like the pumping of a bellows. Her towering vapor jet indicated her distress.

"Instinct tells her to stay close to us, sir," murmured Hudson. "You'd think she was begging us for protection. Could she have sensed that we were her last hope?"

The question was uttered in an odd way that annoyed Clark. He twitted the young lieutenant in his most authoritative voice.

"Don't talk such nonsense, Mr. Hudson. Do you

think the presence of the *Daring* will scare off the orcas? I doubt it, judging from their ferocity."

"Certainly not the *presence alone* of the ship," Bjorg interrupted. "Now they've spotted their prey and are advancing in a half circle."

Stressing the words *presence alone*, he had flashed a defiant, knowing look at the captain. Clark turned away uneasily and noticed that everyone else on the bridge wore the same look. He felt that the entire crew was staring at him expectantly, and those stares, which seemed to carry a plea, made him increasingly nervous.

"Instinct perhaps," murmured Bjorg. "I, for one, believe these animals are highly intelligent, and whales can be amazingly so. I think you guessed right, Mr. Hudson. She understands we are her last chance of survival."

Clark kept silent, sensing that everyone awaited his response. He seemed involved in an intense inner struggle. Lieutenant Hudson became so excited that he found the nerve to say what was on his mind and challenged his superior.

"Sir, when I suggested that the whale figured we were her last hope, I wasn't just thinking of our physical proximity. That's not exactly what I meant to say."

"Well, what *did* you mean to say, Mr. Hudson?" Clark demanded icily. "Please express yourself more clearly."

The young officer reddened. He started to answer, but the idea he was about to put forth suddenly seemed so ridiculous that he couldn't get the words out. So he hung his head and kept silent. Annoyed at the tension around him, Clark struck out angrily in self-defense.

"If you are incapable of expressing yourself coherently," he announced defiantly, "perhaps someone else can do it. Will someone explain how we can help this beast?"

On the bridge and elsewhere, every man aboard shared Hudson's thinking. Clark sensed that his seeming unconcern and apathy were stirring a revolt. Once again he had the preposterous impression that his destroyer had a personality of its own, that it was struggling against a single emotion, that it was at once begging and exhorting him to do something. This kind of conspiracy, with himself as target, weighed heavily on him, and in his overwrought imagination he likened that burden to the whale's monstrous bulk.

As the silence became intolerable, the chief officer took it upon himself to speak for the crew. He was aloof, the kind of man who could be counted on to discuss vital matters dispassionately. He was not about to give up his habits.

"I think I can guess what Hudson meant to say, sir. We have on board a simple means of preventing this butchery. Of course, it would be somewhat contrary to regulations."

The captain had been aware for some time what the men had in mind. Though he pressed for an explanation, down deep he dreaded that it be clearly stated in words.

"The killers are approaching, sir," Bjorg insisted, pointing to the half-circle of orcas closing in on the whale.

"We could take a shot at them, sir," the chief officer proposed in his usual cheerful, almost sprightly voice. "Perfect targets for the gunners. The alert isn't over and they're still at their stations. If you should decide to fire, I'm certain not one of those killers would escape."

"And a blue whale would be saved," Bjorg went on, "a female, which is no small advantage in view of the rarity of this cetacean species, despite all the laws to protect it."

"The artillery officers agree, sir," continued the chief officer. "I've spoken to several and they share my view. It would only take a couple of salvos and..."

"Now, if I were in your shoes, sir..." young Lieutenant Hudson blurted out....

Clark shot him a withering glance. "You are not in my shoes, Mr. Hudson," he snapped. "I don't wish you to be and I would ask you to remain in your own. This ship has only one captain."

The chief officer resumed in a cheerful voice, as if ignoring his chief's outburst. "The gun crews stand ready to fire on command. Gun batteries and automatic weapons are trained on the killers; fire-control computers track their movements. Of course, sir, you are the only captain on board and I know how very heavy a responsibility this decision is."

"There's not a minute to lose," Bjorg pressed him. "Look: the killers are narrowing the circle. They'll attack and dismember this whale just as they did her mate. The next moment will be too late, for they're closing in; if we hit them, we'll hit her too."

"The only captain on board," as his chief officer put it, felt the sweat dampening his forehead. Later, much later, long after the Falklands war was past history, he would recall this last minute as the supremely trying one of all the battles that lay ahead. And by that time a host of unforgettable events would crowd his memory. The destroyer *Daring* was not spared: strafed from the air by machine guns, it went on to become the target of the latest guided missiles designed to hunt down a victim as relentlessly as a bloodhound. It was a miracle the vessel survived: a bomb that pierced the bridge had lodged close to a magazine. Luckily, it failed to explode on impact, but there were agonizing moments while it was being dismantled. These and other perils came with the job of a wartime naval command. Clark's education, training, and repeated practice had drilled him to respond instantly to emergencies. But nothing had prepared him to meet the extraordinary situation he faced as he stood tensely gripping the bridge rail, with the killers below tightening the noose around their prey and his crew staring implacably at him with glaring or pleading eyes.

All well and good for the men to compel him to order something the high command unquestionably would view as sheer insanity. They were not responsible for the ship. They would only obey the order he alone could give. Instantly, the vivid consequences of his decision flashed before him, the waiting avalanche of accusations and reprisals. The admiral was not going to tolerate any whimsy from one of his captains. Clark knew him well enough to predict the worst: the end of his career, cashiered from his command—he, one of the youngest lieutenant commanders in the Royal Navy. And once again, the injustice of having this ordeal thrust upon him was so overwhelming that, in a rush of self-pity, he nearly wept.

He stiffened, clenched his fists, and shot a hateful look at the enormous beast that had chanced to rise out of the ocean to ruin his ambitions. The whale was even nearer now. Bjorg had been right: she was begging for protection and saw the destroyer as her last hope. She was so close that he could see one of her eyes, so ridiculously tiny in proportion to her great bulk, eyes much like human eyes, but very far apart, enabling her to watch the ship while swimming parallel to it. Bjorg had explained to him that because of this peculiar separation of its eyes, the whale cannot see straight ahead but has excellent lateral vision.

This look seemed to focus on him, LCDR Clark, sole master of the ship. No time to request permission; impossible, at any rate, for at best such a request would be treated as a tasteless joke. At worst, they would think him balmy and unfit to command a ship.

Less than thirty seconds left; soon, as Bjorg had warned, it would be too late. Clark straightened his shoulders, drew a deep breath, and made his decision. It was like plunging into uncharted seas bristling with hidden menace. But having at last decided, he felt his burden dissolve as if by magic.

"Fire!" he shouted in a resounding cry of defiance. "Fire at will!"

A wild roar echoed from every combat station, in concert with a lethal hail of ammunition from the latest, most efficient weapons, the pride of Britain's fleet, with which the destroyer *Daring* was amply supplied.

9

THE ARMADA, composed of warships, troop transports, and a great assortment of escort vessels, progressed at the reduced speed adopted upon leaving South Georgia. Reconnaissance craft like the *Daring* rode several miles ahead of the main convoy, out of sight. Apart from the appearance of the whales, which turned out to be a false alarm, the voyage thus far resembled a tranquil cruise. The admiral did not expect any action to develop before their arrival in the vicinity of the Falklands. The only foreseeable trouble might arise if a stray underwater craft happened to elude the surveillance of British nuclear submarines lurking off the Argentine coast. But that, according to all their intelligence sources, was unlikely. The fleet advanced under relatively peaceful skies.

The sudden crash of artillery fire broke the daily routine like a thunderclap and startled every man afloat. The admiral rushed to his command post, where Grant, his chief of staff, had preceded him and was issuing rapid commands. All units of the fleet had their decks cleared for action.

"What the hell's going on, Mr. Grant?" demanded the admiral.

Somewhat embarrassed, the chief of staff had to admit his ignorance. "All I can tell you, sir, is that the destroyer *Daring* has gone into action; I recognize the sound of her guns."

The violent explosions continued in rapid succession. The admiral cocked his ear and listened attentively. From experience he had learned to trust what Grant told him.

"You're right, it *is* the *Daring*. I can hear the booming of her rapid-fire five-inchers. This time, Clark apparently isn't up against a whale. I was right to lecture him on vigilance. What's the purpose of this action? What does Clark say?"

"That's what strikes me as strange, sir. Clark doesn't say a word. No message. Silence from the destroyer."

"What?" the admiral exclaimed in disbelief.

"As I've said, sir, there's no report from the *Daring*. I'd be worried if we hadn't heard her artillery. She can't have been hit seriously; there's no smoke in the air."

"Good Lord! Why haven't you called Clark or his chief officer for an explanation?"

"I did just that, sir, after alerting all units and ordering aircraft to the aid of the *Daring*. They're taking off right now; we've lost no time.... What strikes me as really odd is the communications gap: I haven't been able to contact any officer of rank on the destroyer, only some sheepish subordinates who told me that the lieu-tenant commander and his chief officer were busy but they didn't think the action was anything to worry about."

"What?" roared the admiral, exasperated. "Nothing to worry about when every single five-incher on that ship is peppering the place with shells? And they're busy? No time to waste on such trivial matters as informing the high command? Mr. Grant, you will call upon Clark to explain himself without delay. Tell him I want to speak to him immediately, no matter what the situation is. That's an order."

"Aye, aye, sir."

The chief of staff hurried off to transmit these in-structions and quickly returned. "Order transmitted, sir. I was informed that the lieutenant commander would come to the telephone in a few minutes."

"A few minutes," muttered the admiral, a crimson flush invading his cheeks. "I do not care for this infor-mality, Mr. Grant."

"Nor I, sir, but perhaps he can't leave his post in the midst of the action."

The admiral managed to control his temper and lis-tened attentively once more. The violent explosions of the last few minutes were dying down.

"The five-inch guns are silent, sir, do you hear? Now the machine guns are clattering. I wonder what all this means."

The admiral was torn by perplexity and mounting impatience. The shelling had indeed ended, replaced now by the rapid chatter of automatic weapons.

"Four-millimeter antiaircraft guns, no mistaking the

sound," groaned the admiral. "What the deuce can they be firing at? The only planes aloft are from our own squadron. In any event, no enemy aircraft would dare to venture this far from the Islands."

"They could also be gunning at a target in the water."

"What target?"

Grant was growing more and more vexed, feeling slightly guilty at his own ignorance and frustrated by it, his job being to keep on top of every detail of the whole operation. He hung his head sheepishly in silence.

"We'll get an advance report, sir, while we wait for Clark to fill us in," Grant said at last. "Our planes are circling the destroyer right now. I believe this is the news I urged the squadron commander to send me as soon as possible."

On the telephone he received a lengthy message from the airman, then reappeared before the admiral looking puzzled and contrite.

"Well?"

"Well, sir," he began awkwardly...

In reporting the squadron commander's words, Grant spoke slowly and hesitantly, as if stunned by the information he was transmitting and dreading the reaction it was sure to provoke.

"Well, sir, good news first. No one has spotted the enemy: no plane, no ship, no submarine. That's of crucial importance."

"What they didn't see is of no interest," growled the admiral. "They must have seen something, right?"

"I'm getting to that, sir. What struck them to begin with was the color of the water around the *Daring*. Red, blood-red. The flight commander couldn't believe his eyes. There was blood spread out in a semicircle for more than a quarter of a mile around the ship."

"A sea of blood?" the admiral exclaimed in horror. "For that there'd have to be hundreds of casualties. And you tell me they saw no foes."

"That was my first response, sir, out of anxiety. The pilot reassured me. He saw no bodies, no human bodies, that is."

"*Human* bodies? What does that mean, Mr. Grant?"

"It means that he flew over a mass of dead or dying sea creatures—marine animals if you like, sir. He took them to be sharks, but mammoth ones, the likes of which he'd never seen. Some were still thrashing about in that bloody water, but most were floating belly-up. Swarms of them, sir. He couldn't even start to count them but said there must have been more than a hundred. And over the dead and dying bodies the shells were still falling."

Grant had every reason to dread the admiral's reaction. While he was talking, the familiar signs appeared warning that the admiral's wrath, like a seething caldron, was about to boil over: his brow darkened and his face turned crimson; the veins in his neck bulged alarmingly. As he listened to his chief of staff, the admiral began to think that some spiteful demon had pumped out the brains of every member of his sea and air forces, that he was now in charge of a legion of lunatics instead of honest, loyal subjects of Her Majesty the Queen.

"Are you telling me the destroyer unleashed her full

firepower at a bunch of sharks?" he finally sputtered.

"That seems to be what the squadron commander has reported, sir. He observed very particularly the impact of the columns of water raised by each burst of gunfire. On sharks and only on sharks."

"No enemy other than sharks?" shouted the admiral. "That's all?"

"That's about it, sir. No, I forgot. One other observation."

"Like the last one?"

"Something like it, sir. A whale."

"A whale!" the admiral bellowed. "I should have guessed we hadn't seen the end of those filthy beasts. What about this whale?"

"Alive, sir, and apparently enormous. It swims a cable's length or two from the destroyer and follows the same course. Shells and bullets don't seem to have affected it... Oh, yes, the pilot made one final observation."

"You don't say, Mr. Grant. A final observation, was it?"

"A body larger than a shark's, also mangled and bleeding, sort of a shapeless carcass, but well behind the battlefield. The pilot thinks it's an enormous whale half eaten by voracious fish."

The meaning of these assorted bits and pieces slowly began to emerge in the admiral's mind. Hadn't Clark signaled the presence of a pair of whales? Yet the truth seemed too extravagant to accept. He was silent for the longest time, while Grant went on dreading his reactions.

They were dignified. His terrible temper occasionally took the form not of an explosion but of something much worse: studied calm.

"Mr. Grant," he said at last in an icy voice, "I must assume, despite all appearances, that our squadron commander has not suddenly lost his senses—a kind of air sickness, perhaps? I must also assume that you yourself are mentally fit, that you heard no extraterrestrial voices on the telephone, and that you faithfully communicated the pilot's message."

"You can be sure of it, sir."

"Then will you tell me quietly, if that is still possible, whether you reach the same conclusion as I, or whether the admiral commanding this force is the one who's losing his mind?"

"Sir," Grant replied hesitantly, "I have to admit the whole business is extravagant, but I can see only one possible explanation: the destroyer fired on the sharks."

"That's my belief. And why?"

"To save the second whale," murmured the chief of staff in a barely audible whisper.

"That's roughly the conclusion I have reached," whispered the admiral. "And can you see any valid reason for such conduct?"

Grant shook his head by way of reply. The admiral was about to comment further when a telephone call from the *Daring's* captain was announced. Scarcely able to control a nervous twitch, he hesitated.

"Take the call," he told his chief of staff. "I don't think I could talk to him at the moment."

While Grant was gone, he paced the deck, stern-faced, silent. He gazed indifferently at the returning reconnaissance planes as they landed, but turned his back on the squadron commander who came forward to confirm his report. In response to the unfriendly welcome, the airman did not persist and walked away. A few minutes later Grant returned.

"Well?"

"Well, sir, it seems that both of us were right basically, though a number of details are different. Those were not sharks but orcas, rapacious animals that hunt in packs when they prey on whales. They're called killers and they were after the two whales. They butchered one, as you guessed; the flyers saw its carcass. Apparently they were attacking its mate, the female, when Clark gave the order to fire. He told me a whole long story to justify his act, kind of a rambling recital. He seemed all excited and not very proud of what he'd done. I took some notes so as not to forget anything. First..."

"Spare me the details, please; basic facts will do for the moment. I'll wait to hear the rest from his own lips, this lieutenant commander of the Royal Navy, this valorous captain who never hesitated to unleash a ten-minute barrage of fire on sharks or other marine animals when we are at war. God help us! Mr. Grant, I hope you gave him to understand that I am not at all satisfied with his actions."

"I believe I conveyed the appropriate observations, sir. I made it clear that you were deeply disturbed."

"Disturbed, eh?" growled the admiral. "What did he say?"

"He asked me to apologize for him, sir. He's on the

phone now, waiting to report to you. He said he was prepared to accept your discipline."

"Discipline, ha!" roared the admiral, "when I'm ready to hang him from the mast as an example! Well, you can tell him to wait and see me this evening. I'll send a helicopter to pick him up. I haven't the patience to deal with the matter right now; if I were to talk to him at this moment he'd shortly blow his brains out or take a dive into the icy water, which wouldn't help the situation. . . . No, come to think of it, I want to see for myself what's going on aboard that ship. Tell him I will make an inspection tomorrow morning around ten. It will probably take me the whole night to calm down. Oh, and tell him to forget the ceremony when I come; this might be the time to remind him that we're at war. And be sure to warn him," he continued, a note of menace creeping into his voice, "that I expect a precise account, down to every last shell and cartridge, of the ammunition wasted in that senseless display of fireworks against the sharks."

"Orcas, sir."

"All right, orcas. It makes no difference, do you understand?"

"Aye, aye, sir."

"Orcas!" the admiral repeated, rolling his eyes hopelessly. "This war, Mr. Grant, is off to a lunatic start."

10

ABOARD the destroyer *Daring* the shelling and shooting had gone on far longer than was necessary to cripple the orca assault. A murderous rage seemed to grip the gun crews, a lust for revenge unfulfilled until the last of the killers was dead. Leaning on the bridge railing, lost in a daze, Clark never thought to halt the firing. Every weapon aboard had come into action, one rivaling another for speed and accuracy. Just as the admiral had said, the five-inch guns had opened the festivities with superb results where the orcas were densely packed. Next, the antiaircraft guns had their say, dispatching the wounded in rapid order. Even the fire-control technicians seemed to share in the general exuberance, reading their instruments with unwonted zeal and precision.

The telephone had rung several times. Neither Clark nor his chief officer seemed to hear it, so entranced were they by the sight of the scarlet sea that made such an impression on the pilots. Clark scarcely budged when an orderly appeared, announcing a phone call from the command ship. His blank stare was riveted on the whale, blind agent of this bold and perilous venture.

For the whale was still there on the starboard side, a cable's length behind the destroyer, rolling along effortlessly in what might have passed for a victory dance, unperturbed by the roaring guns. The peculiar mechanics of her visual system permitted her to watch the welcome slaughter of her foes out of her right eye and the bridge on the friendly destroyer with the left one, in which, according to Bjorg, there shone a gleam of infinite gratitude.

"She understands, sir," he kept repeating to Clark. "The intelligence of these animals is astounding."

An officer came to inform the captain of another urgent telephone call. "The Admiral himself is asking for you, sir. It's an order, I'm told by the chief of staff."

Clark tried to rouse himself out of his stupor. Nodding his head in resignation, he glanced glumly at the sky where the planes were still circling, ordered a cease fire, and made his way dejectedly to the telephone.

His two conversations with Grant left no doubt as to how the high command viewed his conduct. Not that he had any illusions on that score. Still, it was a relief to hear that the admiral didn't want to see him until the following morning: the respite would give him a chance to collect his thoughts. He spent the rest of the day reliving the destruction of the orcas, rehearsing it for the admiral's ears, and also trying to figure out what had compelled him to indulge in an act so patently extravagant.

"Extravagant" and "extravagance" were the words droning in the admiral's head when, after a restless night, accompanied only by an aide, he was deposited by helicopter on the deck of the *Daring*. According to instructions, a single row of sailors was there to present arms.

Clark saluted crisply. The admiral responded with a rapid, careless flick of his hand, then scowled at the men presenting arms and swept the bridge with a searching glance. If he had expected to find evidence of laxity and disorder in the ship's appearance—the signal for him to raise the roof—he would have been a poor psychologist. The lieutenant commander's salute (a salute straight out of the military manual) as well as the men's impeccable alignment and presentation of arms could have served as models for all units in the Royal Navy, and even the Horse Guards. Their uniforms, too, were beyond reproach. Having re-established his authority the day before, Clark had given strict orders for the ship and its crew to be scrubbed and shining. They were unnecessary. The sailors knew there was trouble brewing, and even if the responsibility was in no way theirs, they still felt a mild ache of collective guilt. The threat of punishment did not affect them, for they had merely obeyed orders; but the fact that they had helped to influence their skipper's decision—for which he alone would have to answer—filled them with a vague sense of remorse. They had spent part of the night chasing away dust, polishing the brightwork to a sparkling finish even under gray skies, and rubbing down the gun barrels until the insides shone.

But the admiral had no intention of performing an arms inspection; he left that to the officer accompanying him. Immediately on arrival he had noted the tidiness and cleanliness—exceptional even in the navy—of the deck and the crew. It was a satisfying sight, he had to admit. Knowing from experience the amount of work and care it involved, he could scarcely supress a smirk of pleasure. But that sensation was short-lived: he hadn't come aboard the *Daring* to hand out laurels. Scowling again, he informed Clark in a voice of doom that he wished to speak to him privately.

"Aye, aye, sir."

As the lieutenant commander led the way to his office, at the admiral's request, the latter gave a sudden start.

"What's that?"

About a hundred yards off the starboard side he had seen the colossal, undulating back of a marine animal whose wake nearly equalled the destroyer's.

With exaggerated coolness Clark replied, "That? Oh, it's a whale, sir."

The same way he might have said: It's a butterfly fluttering around us, or, it's a sea gull that won't let us out of its sight; a tone of voice that at first sounded flippant to the admiral but that he quickly recognized as sheer embarrassment.

"A whale? Is it one of those your radar picked up?"

"Indeed it is, sir; also the one that caused this untimely incident."

"Untimely!" snapped the admiral. "You certainly choose your words. We will have to discuss this later. Now, it seems that this whale is following you?"

"Since yesterday, like a bloodhound, sir; she stayed on our heels throughout the night," Clark declared bitterly. "It seems she won't let us out of her sight."

At times he felt the whale's constant presence was a specter sent to haunt him and remind him of his disgrace.

"Doesn't it sleep at night?"

"Since this type of cetacean has been known to accompany a ship for several days, sir, some naturalists have inferred that whales never sleep. At least that's what Bjorg told me."

"You mean the former whaler you brought aboard, who knows the Falklands like the palm of his hand?"

"Yes, sir. He knows everything there is to know about cetaceans. He taught me a lot about blue whales."

"Taught you a lot, did he indeed?" snarled the admiral, moving on after one last inquisitive, puzzled look at the beast.

It was true. The whale seemed reluctant to part company from the ship. In their leisure moments, officers and crewmen would check to make sure of this. The look on their faces alternated between sulking resentment, like Clark's, and jubilation, derived perhaps from the pleasure of having carried out a tricky assignment, as if their sense of guilt found release in the endless contortions of this gigantic, vibrant body.

11

THE ADMIRAL entered Clark's office, sat down, and invited the owner to do likewise. Curiously, he no longer felt the smoldering anger he counted on to help him dress down this officer. Annoyed at himself for having lost the impetus, he tried to rekindle his righteous wrath without quite knowing where to find a match. Thinking he had the answer, he demanded snappishly whether Clark had prepared an account of the ammunition wasted the day before during the regrettable incident. Clark handed him a list. The admiral glanced at it briefly, shrugged his shoulders, and came to the point.

"Do you realize, Mr. Clark, the needless expense you have incurred because of your rash decision? Have you any idea what your squandered ammunition is going to cost the British taxpayer?"

It was an unpromising start and a feeble argument,

as the admiral quickly realized, regretting his lack of imagination. Inwardly, he winced to think Clark could have countered that his act cost little compared to the whole Falklands operation and amounted to a very minimal increase in an individual's tax bill. However, the officer remained silent and contrite; thankful for this, the admiral continued, his voice less grating.

"Are you aware of the anxiety and commotion you caused throughout the fleet: decks cleared for action, an air squadron sent aloft?"

"I'm aware of it, sir," the lieutenant commander stammered. "I'm sorry; I'd like to apologize."

"Can you give me a rational explanation for such conduct?"

"After seeing the first whale savagely torn apart—butchered—I thought it would be unfair to let the same thing happen to the other poor animal, whose life we saved and who seems to have placed herself under our protection. I alone had the means to prevent another killing."

"And do you consider," bawled the admiral, his anger teetering on the brink of a new explosion, "do you consider it the duty of the captain of a destroyer, whose every concern ought to focus on a possible encounter with an enemy submarine, to rush to the aid of an animal with a pyrotechnic display that must have resounded for miles around, while the fleet is advancing with extreme caution? I had the impression—and your list confirms it—that you didn't spare the five-inch shells. Really, now, I might have accepted..."

Annoyed at himself for showing signs of weakness, he stopped, corrected himself, and completed his sentence with a shrug. "I might have understood, not accepted, machine-gun fire—out of pity. Don't you think that would have sufficed?"

"Totally insufficient, sir," Clark replied, his face suddenly brightening, "because the killers were too numerous and too rapacious."

"Killers?"

"That's what they call orcas. Killer whales, or just killers."

"What surprises me, Mr. Clark," the admiral resumed with crushing sarcasm, "is that you never saw fit to launch one of your torpedoes at those whale-eaters you call killers. I am truly astonished."

"I thought it was unnecessary, sir," Clark replied in the same confident tone. "Unnecessary and futile. The target was not compact enough to justify the use of torpedoes. The situation called for dispersed fire from many sources; as it turned out, the scattered shelling proved effective."

He was talking like a referee at the close of target practice. Confronting what appeared to be a pillar of artless candor, the admiral felt tongue-tied. Clark seized the opportunity to plead his cause with mounting fervor and conviction. He described indignantly the ruthless butchering of the first whale, how the killers assaulted their prey with savage cruelty, devouring it even before it was dead.

"Also, sir, you have to imagine how we were feeling.

We'd been through an agonizing half-hour, as you know, and all kinds of mental torture each time we recalled Prince Philip's warning, but at least we had the satisfaction of rescuing this one poor creature. Then to think all our efforts might go down the drain!"

"You are highly impressionable, Mr. Clark. I'm not persuaded that such sensitivity is the best qualification for a naval officer in wartime."

"I wasn't the only one in that frame of mind, sir. My officers and men were just as upset as I. The gun crews had set their sights on that pack of killers. They were all begging me to do something; I felt the ship herself was summoning me to give the command."

Momentarily stunned by all this, the admiral frowned again.

"I take it you subscribe to that well-known quip by some European, 'I was their leader; I had to follow them.'?"

"It's not that, sir. I realized they would have resented it if I hadn't given the command to fire; what really drove me to it, though, was the thought that I would have hated myself if I hadn't done it then and there. Once the firing began, I felt a great load off my back. Finally, no matter what the consequences are for me—and I considered them at the outset of this whole incident—I have to admit that what I said a moment ago isn't true. I don't regret my decision."

He had nothing more to say. The admiral, whose irritation had given way to musing, understood and ended the meeting.

"Allow me to ask what I should do, sir," Clark ventured as they returned to the deck. "Should I consider myself under detention? I'm prepared to pay the price."

"That's all you can think of," growled the admiral, flaring up again to cover his confusion. "Do you insist on dictating what I should do? I'll think about it and let you know my decision in due time. Meanwhile, try to behave like a ship's captain instead of the knight champion of all whales."

The admiral remained tight-lipped during his return to the carrier. He listened without comment to the report of his aide, who declared the destroyer to be in immaculate order. Equally laconic was his response to the quizzical look of his chief of staff as he stepped from the helicopter.

"Muddled explanations. The whole story is fuzzy. I'll have to think about it further."

Grant did not pursue the subject when his superior lapsed into gloomy silence. Before leaving, he asked:

"Should I mention the incident to the top brass, sir?"

"Not just yet. What will happen if you submit a report?"

A note of sadness crept into the chief of staff's voice. "If Clark hasn't been able to justify his actions, sir, I don't see how we can avoid a court-martial."

The admiral stared at him intently, as if he had uttered something outrageous.

"What's that you say, Mr. Grant? Kindly repeat what you just said. I didn't catch it."

Abashed, the chief of staff stammered, "I said, sir, at least I meant to say: I don't see how we can avoid a court-martial."

"That's what I thought I heard and it surprised me," the admiral retorted aggressively. "For several reasons. First, why should Clark be court-martialed? On grounds of disobedience? You who know the naval code by heart, can you cite me a single article dealing with such a case?"

Grant thought a moment and conceded there was no such clause.

"There you are!... What's more," the admiral continued glibly, "if this were a case for court-martial—this is just a guess, mind you, a random guess—why the devil should we protect LCDR Clark? Can you give me one good reason?"

"I was just thinking aloud, sir," Grant apologized.

"The truth is that we have an exceptional case on our hands. It's up to us to deal imaginatively with it."

Having had his say, the admiral shut the door of his cabin and returned to his solitary, comfortless meditation.

What he had said to Grant merely expressed his state of mind. Actually, he felt twinges of the same bewilderment that Clark had experienced under totally different conditions. Like Clark, he had to face a unique situation, had to deal with a problem he had never run up against before. "A unique situation," he reflected. "Even the military experts can't give me sensible advice."

Having reached this conclusion, he invited over his off-duty advisers, the padre and Dr. Hodges, and told them the whole story in a voice either trembling with fury or perturbed and faintly sympathetic.

12

His two friends listened attentively, the padre with half-shut eyes, the neurologist with evident professional interest.

"By the way," the admiral added, after recounting the facts, "I saw the whale. That devilish beast seems to have attached itself to the destroyer—follows it around like a dog."

"Instinctive gratitude," Hodges commented. "Characteristic of certain animals, it's been observed."

"Is it a beautiful creature?" the padre inquired.

"Very beautiful, undeniably so," the admiral responded with unexpected alacrity and conviction. "Impressive size; at least a hundred feet long."

"No serious wounds?"

"Apparently not. It wriggles about like a gudgeon, if you see what I mean."

"Well, there's one solid fact at least," said the padre softly.

"A significant one," the doctor emphasized.

The admiral stared at them both in surprise, but made no comment. He kept silent because he was eager to know their opinions.

"I suppose you expect a neurologist's diagnosis from me, sir?" Hodges said. "You want to know whether I think this officer is mad, or at least if he's stable enough to command a warship in wartime."

"That's about it," grumbled the admiral. "You must admit, Doc, such behavior isn't normal in a naval officer."

"Some naval officers behave far more oddly, sir."

"That's news to me. Do you know any?"

"I can assure you they're not immune from temporary or permanent mental disorders. As a matter of fact, I suspect that long stretches at sea reinforce the power of the imagination."

"Thanks for them and for me, Doc," growled the admiral.

"For my own amusement, sir, I kept a little notebook of eccentric behavior in certain individuals; some were cases I treated, others were reported to me. You'll find a few surprises in it."

"For example?" the admiral pressed him, always eager to hear an anecdote about the navy and its men.

"The most interesting tale is probably the one about a fellow named Shrapnel, captain of a British warship, the *Haughty*, who took it upon himself to drop anchor in 1896 off the Cocos Islands where a fabulous legendary treasury was supposed to lie buried. His visions of this treasure fired Shrapnel's imagination and unsettled his mind. Unofficially, and with nobody's blessing but his own, he sent the crew ashore to begin the search, 'borrowed' some dynamite from the ship's magazine, and set the men to work, stripped to the waist, with pick and shovel, while he directed operations on the strength of a compass and a dubious map probably drawn by a worse crackpot than himself. The work went on for a week, after which the *Haughty* headed for home empty-handed and Captain Shrapnel had to explain himself to his superiors."

"Interesting," the admiral responded cheerfully, forgetting for a moment the problem at hand. "Lend me your notebook, will you, Doc? Whatever happened to the treasure hunter?"

"The Admiralty demanded his resignation, and he obliged."

"No way around it," sighed the admiral. "Getting back to our problem, what do you think of Clark?"

"Bears no resemblance to Shrapnel's situation," the doctor protested. "Shrapnel acted out of self-interest: he was after treasure. Clark's case is different. Also, the other fellow had planned his move and the adventure lasted over a week, whereas Clark had to make a decision on the spot.... No, all things considered, I'm sure he's not crazy and I don't even think his behavior suggests an anxiety complex. He acted under the pressure of extraordinary events. Remember, he had to make a choice in a matter of seconds, having just undergone a period of extreme stress. He was forced to choose either to do nothing, to let things happen, or to take action against a foe, which the killers represented at that moment. Can you fault a young officer for vigorous action in wartime? I don't believe so."

"That strikes me as an odd way to look at the business," the admiral muttered. "But it's your opinion. How do you feel about it, Padre?"

"I know nothing about military matters, Admiral."

"That's why I want your advice."

"I do think, however, that I'm qualified to judge his sins. Was a great deal of ammunition wasted by Clark's action? Did it create a shortage for your fleet?"

The admiral shrugged and had to admit that the loss was insignificant. A minor maneuver would use up far more ammunition, and the opening battle of the Falklands was bound to consume even more.

"But that's not the question, Padre."

"It counts, nevertheless, in my view. Must we not measure sin in relation to the amount of harm it causes?"

"That's only part of it."

"Yes, of course; there is also the intent. In this particular case it seems to me that the intent was not evil."

"I can guess what you're going to tell me: that the intent was admirable."

"Nobody can condemn it, not even you, Admiral. In this instance I very much doubt there was any sin involved."

"You can't argue with a churchman," grumbled the admiral.

"Not when you're talking about sin," Hodges added.

The combined opinions of these two advisers and friends had reinforced an attitude the admiral had already flirted with after visiting the destroyer and spending an hour in thought. Was it right to blemish, or even to cut off, so promising a career? Clark was an officer on the rise, slated shortly for promotion. Puzzled and distressed, the admiral asked himself this question to discover whether he was becoming softhearted or simply human.

"I'm convinced that every man aboard these ships would welcome a gesture of clemency on your part, sir," Hodges declared. "The men would resent a show of harshness."

"You really think so?"

"I'm sure of it. From the top ranks down to the ordinary deckhand. Ask the orderly who shines your boots."

"I won't do any such thing," the admiral protested. "If I did that I'd be the butt of that familiar quip, 'I was their leader; I had to follow them.'"

"Aren't we a democratic nation?" asked the padre.

"Sir," the doctor said, "doesn't the morale of these sailors and their respect for their leader enter into the balance sheet of successful future operations?"

The admiral remained silent, thinking. He felt more and more unsure of himself.

"What if I decided to forget the whole thing," he said at last. "Not that I'm going to, you understand, but if I simply were to overlook this lunacy, what should I do? I can't conceal the fact that we opened fire; everyone heard the shelling. The destroyer's logbook and our own will record the fact. A moment ago my chief of staff told me he couldn't see how we could avoid a court-martial. I'll admit he didn't sound happy about it."

Hodges spoke up. "There you are, your chief of staff—a stickler for discipline if ever there was one—doesn't favor harsh treatment."

"As to the *how* of his comment," the padre added softly, "Grant, whose admirable merits I'm the first to applaud, seems to have lacked imagination in the present case. If you can't overlook the gunfire, can't you fudge a little as to the target? Say, for example, h-m-m... that the radar had spotted an unidentified ship that failed to respond to our signals. After repeated challenges, say, the lieutenant commander sent several shots over her bow, which is perfectly normal, just a warning. H-m-m... then when the destroyer advanced, it found a wreck, an abandoned fishing boat, h-m-m... a whaling boat, how about that? I'm no seaman, but I know such things have happened. There are so many shipwrecks in this storm-tossed ocean... they're actually a hazard to navigation and shouldn't be left afloat. Under those conditions Clark decided to keep on firing in order to sink the wreck and get it out of the way. Simple as that. No one can blame him for what he did."

The admiral eyed the padre with wonder. "Maybe we ought to propose him for a decoration! Padre, if my chief of staff lacks resourcefulness, you certainly make up for it."

"Does your Bible study inspire these flights of fancy?" Hodges inquired, looking just as amazed as the admiral.

"Do the seminaries stress development of the imagination?"

"I have a tendency to daydream," the chaplain confessed mildly. "It's not a mortal sin as long as it doesn't get out of hand. Maybe I've done so this time. Does my version of the facts seem absurd, Admiral? Isn't it plausible?"

"Plausible, plausible, perhaps. You know you're suggesting that I write a false report, an act of treason. If you were a Catholic priest, Padre, I would lump you with those confounded Jesuits! I note your interpretation of the facts, only there's one small problem. Not just the ship's logbook; not just the written accounts you want me to falsify; I'm certain that right now, in addition to the crew of the *Daring,* many other seamen suspect what really happened. Later on they're bound to talk; then what will I look like?"

The padre said nothing. Dr. Hodges assumed the task of demolishing this latest objection.

"On that point I can put your mind at ease, sir. As you suggest, the slaughter of the orcas is now common knowledge throughout the fleet. I can even promise you there isn't a single sailor aboard this or any other ship who couldn't recite the whole adventure blow by blow. Radio operators use their own secret communications code between official messages. Well, everyone applauds Clark's conduct and hopes he won't be punished. They're not likely to talk."

"You think so?"

"I'm sure of it. There's a journalist on board, right? Well, he really has no idea what happened. He's the only one. He knows there was artillery and machine-gun fire from the *Daring*, but that's all. Not a single sailor filled him in."

"How can you be so sure?"

"I, for my part, often chat with my orderly," said Hodges, making a slight bow.

"Well?"

"We had a long conversation this morning, so I'm aware what the bluejackets in this fleet are thinking."

"Thank you both for your helpful advice," the admiral concluded with a sly smile. "I think I'm sufficiently informed now to be able to deal with the incident in a satisfactory manner."

13

Having decided that he had spent enough time thinking and talking about a whale, the admiral went into action to settle the matter forthwith. The first person to learn of his decision was his chief of staff.

"We were both wrong, Mr. Grant," he declared casually. "We were deceived by appearances. My conversation with Clark cleared up everything. Nothing like personal contact, I've always said. The captain of the *Daring* has done nothing wrong. He fired at a shipwreck that was a navigational hazard and sank it."

He proceeded to recite the padre's imaginary version of events, adding details from his own experience at sea to make it more authentic. Startled at the outset, Grant soon was listening with a mixture of awe and exhilaration.

"Appearances indeed are often deceiving, sir. I probably misunderstood what Clark was saying over the phone. Surely he was all keyed up by the alert and he may have expressed himself awkwardly."

"Must have been that."

"One thing, sir: we ought to make sure that the tensions of the moment haven't prompted Clark to record a different version from ours in the logbook. I presume our account will not mention the nature of the actual incident."

"Excellent point; you're right. Get Clark on the phone for me... Anything else?" he added, noting Grant's hesitation.

"The squadron commander is sure to make his report also, sir."

"You think of everything, Mr. Grant. You are a model chief of staff. I'll talk to him as soon as I'm through with Clark."

The admiral got through by phone to the lieutenant commander.

"I've been thinking," he began. "I can't fault you for anything. It's quite natural for you to have fired a warning across the bow of a ship that refused to answer your challenge, natural that you decided to sink a wreck posing a threat to navigation."

"Beg pardon, sir?"

"I said: a wreck posing a threat to navigation," roared the admiral. "Can't you hear me? It's perfectly plain. I'll repeat..."

As the admiral recited the official version of events, the officer's face slowly lit up. He was on the verge of tears by the time he heard the full story, which the provident chief of staff had padded with enough meaty substance to convince even the most critical listener.

"Aye, aye, sir," Clark stammered at the close of this remarkable exposition. "My logbook will set things straight."

"Let's hope so," growled the admiral, and hung up. ..."Now for the squadron commander."

It was not his style to telephone instructions to his officers. Generally, his staff took care of that, but the whale affair had grown too important to be delegated to subordinates.

"Commander," he began reprovingly to the pilot, "I wish to give you some advice."

"Me, sir?"

"Oh, I'm not blaming you for anything. In the fog that blankets these bloody waters I know it's easy to imagine all sorts of apparitions and to, let's say, miss the forest for the trees. On the telephone you reported sharks. Now, there may have been some sharks or other marine animals around; we all know these seas are full of them. But you never identified the target of the destroyer's fire. I don't recall your saying a word about that wreck."

The squadron commander in turn was treated to a full-dress recital of the official story, which by now had accumulated a few more picturesque trappings. The admiral finished his tale only to be greeted with a resounding silence, which so annoyed him that he exploded.

"Well, why don't you say something? Speak up, for God's sake!"

At last the pilot replied in a steady voice. "Sir, I say nothing because I'm puzzled. I was too unsure of the facts to mention the shipwreck. Most of it probably had sunk by the time I flew over the field of action and, as you pointed out, there was a lot of fog as well as smoke. But now that I think of it, I do seem to recall something like the tip of a ship's mast just as it was sinking. I didn't speak of it because it didn't seem important, but I'll be sure to include it in my written report."

"Be sure you do," replied the admiral, relieved, then added, "you know you're devilishly clever for an airman!"

"Thank you, sir."

"Next time, however, don't be too clever," he concluded gruffly.

Replacing the receiver, he sighed and poured himself a double shot of whiskey, something he rarely did before sundown. It was almost lunchtime. Instead of his usual quick snack alone, today he had invited the padre and the doctor to join him, so he went up on deck for a brisk walk to work up an appetite.

He felt unsure of himself—for him, an unfamiliar state of mind: one moment he was relieved to have settled the whole matter, only to feel guilty the next, as if he had committed a crime by covering up an unpardonable misdeed. Despite Hodges' assurances, he dreaded to think how his subordinates would judge a lapse he himself could not excuse. He was afraid to face his officers, not to mention the crew.

His fears soon vanished. The first person he met on deck was a deckhand who was waxing the mounting of an antiaircraft gun. The admiral paced the deck, hands clasped behind his back, head hunched, filled with anxiety—a novelty for him—lest he have to face the blue-jacket's scornful gaze. But the sailor snapped to attention, his crisp salute conveying a hint of veneration, his eyes reassuringly bright and eager. A petty officer came by and reacted similarly, further dissipating the admiral's apprehension. The admiral's heart sang for joy: he answered the salutes with a smile, also uncommon for him.

He wanted to settle matters and to sound out the crew. Alone, he was seen visiting various parts of the carrier. Wherever he went, officers and crewmen greeted him with customary respect, which now bore a tinge of deference and even warmth. His descent into the ship's bowels on his last stop confirmed what Hodges had said: first, just as he had suspected, there were invisible, intangible bonds linking each cell of the fleet, and every decision of the high command, from the most critical to the commonplace, spread instantly; also—and this gladdened him—he learned that his own decision concerning Clark had gained overwhelming approval. In fact, it was so highly esteemed that the secret on which it depended was certain to be jealously guarded by every seaman.

Having discovered this for himself and obtained peace of mind, and feeling more confident that he had probably acted honorably, the admiral greeted his two lunch guests and told them of his satisfaction.

"If dear old Philip ever finds out what I've gone through for a blue whale," he said, "I doubt that even he would reproach me."

Screwing one eyebrow into a slight frown, he added, "I still can't get over the fact that to settle this whale business it took the combined, and perhaps culpable, efforts of an admiral, his chief of staff, an air squadron commander—in fact, the whole fleet."

"Aided by scientific diagnosis," murmured the padre, with a slight bow in the doctor's direction.

"And blessed by the highest spiritual powers," added the neurologist, returning the courtesy.

PART TWO

1

THE BLUE whale escorted, and more often preceded the *Daring*, clearing a passage through southern seas for the convoy of nearly seventy ships packed with tough and tested fighting men, all eager to have a go at the enemy. She had elected to act as ship's scout; she seemed to enjoy the companionship of the destroyer and made every effort to be friendly. Perhaps in her whale's mind she felt grateful to these latter-day knights who had rescued her from an ugly fate. That was Bjorg's impression, and Clark felt inclined to agree as he watched her cavorting alongside the ship.

"In her own way she wants to show that she understands and thanks us," said the former whaler.

Certainly she put on a spectacular show for the appreciative seamen, twisting and turning and rolling like some gigantic Chinese dragon. With her flippers, which Bjorg called her "paddles," she would slap the water furiously as if to call attention to the performance she was about to present.* Surfing through the waves, she would dive shallowly, her tail standing erect for an instant like a lonely sentinel on the water. Then she vanished, only to surface moments later with a sudden thrust of her muscular rib cage and crown her choreographic fantasy by spouting a jet three stories high, which, on windless days, fell back around her like leafy drapery spilling from some prodigious tree, or, when the wind was up and the *Daring* close by, sprayed the destroyer's deck. This greatly amused the sailors, who never thought to rush for cover but greeted the dousing as if it were holy water.

"Some say the vapor jet is harmful, even lethal," Bjorg told Clark. "Superstitious tommyrot. Whale literature is full of old wives' tales. You can see there's no truth in it, at least not so far as our whale is concerned. This one, I predict, will bring us good luck."

Most of the sailors on the *Daring* agreed. As a matter of fact, they began to feel the blue whale was their mascot, a guardian angel shielding them from the ocean's perils.

This feeling pervaded other units of the fleet, for however great the whale's personal affection for the *Daring*, she would turn back frequently and regularly to visit the whole flotilla. She was welcome wherever she went. The sailors christened her Auntie Margot.

---

*An allusion to the practice in the French theater of striking the boards three times with a staff (paddle) to silence the audience before the curtain rises.

Auntie Margot seemed to have forgotten all about her mate's unhappy end. Bearing her widowhood lightly, she regaled the men with lavish entertainments, displaying an infinite assortment of undulations, plunges, and surprise appearances.

On special occasions—a rare treat since she must have kept it for her show-stopper—the whale would dive deep to gain momentum and stay under longer than usual, then rise swiftly and catapult herself straight up out of the water. Standing at Clark's side the first time he watched this astounding demonstration, Bjorg was thrilled.

"My God! I never dreamed she could do that! Like a lot of other whalermen, I was under the misimpression that only sperm whales could hurl themselves vertically like a projectile. She's breaching, sir! She's breaching!"

"She's what?"

"That's what it's called: 'the infinitely wonderful phenomenon of the breach,' as Melville described it. And he couldn't resist quoting a passage from *Moby Dick*, a book that had enchanted him from his boyhood days, parts of which he knew by heart.

"It's about the supernatural appearance of the diabolical white whale, sir. Listen: 'Springing up from the deepest ocean, the cachalot leaps free into the fresh air, heaping up a mountain of glistening foam and marking its position for a distance of seven miles and beyond. At such times the torn, angry waves he tosses about seem to form his mane.' With a whale a hundred feet long, the sight is even more spectacular."

"Breathtaking," the lieutenant commander agreed.

At first the whale's movements had caused some problems. Radar technicians in the tracking station belowdecks were alarmed to find spots hopping about wildly on the screen, but soon they got used to the jerks and twitches. They learned to identify at a glance Auntie Margot's joyful somersaults and, being shut away deep in the ship and unable to enjoy the live show, they took what pleasure they could from the trembling patterns on the bright screen.

At the start, the admiral had viewed these exhibitions with a jaundiced eye, fearing they would distract the men from their real task of maintaining preparedness against enemy attack. On the contrary, as his officers hastened to point out, the antics were generating good humor and a cheerful attitude by having the monotony of the long voyage broken. He found this to be true in many little ways, not the least of which was the indisputable fact that the whale's generous schedule of performances did more to boost shipboard morale than double-feature movies. When Hodges also endorsed this view, the admiral gave up the notion of banning whale-watching. Sometimes he watched too, at first out of curiosity, then with pleasure. In any event, the only way he could have stopped it would have been to pump the animal full of shells, which he was scarcely inclined to do. Short of stirring a mutiny, it would have bred harsh feelings throughout the fleet and caused a scandal back in England. So he resigned himself stoically to the blue whale's presence, assuming she would turn tail and flee at the first hint of enemy action.

The general in command of land forces was among those who saw a real advantage in Auntie Margot's thrilling acrobatics. His soldiers needed distraction far more than the sailors, and her first appearance, like a fairy godmother's, had dissolved the men's deep gloom. They cheered and applauded her every caper.

"She's rolling! She's leaping! She's sounding! She's spouting! She's breaching!"

By now the vocabulary of whaling was on everyone's tongue, thanks to the invisible ties linking the units in a convoy.

The general had assured the admiral that the whale's effect on the men's morale was as good as, if not better than, the swaying hips of the sexiest night-club singers hired to entertain troops during the Korean War.

"My Gurkhas really go for her," he declared. "She's made them forget how homesick they were for their mountains when they first stepped aboard."

One segment of the expeditionary force was, in fact, a small band of Gurkhas, an advance guard later to be reinforced by several thousand more of these mountain folk. They greeted the whale with noisy clamor in a language nobody else could understand, but Auntie Margot seemed to appreciate it so much that sometimes she obliged with an encore.

Having thus displayed her talents and unveiled her charms to the other members of the fleet, the blue whale would slip back silently through the water to the *Daring*, whose crew, anxious over her prolonged absence, welcomed her with shouts of joy. For a few moments she swam alongside the ship, then forged ahead of the convoy to take up her self-appointed post as vigilant scout spearheading the armada of the fierce fighting men pledged to recapture the Falkland Islands.

2

THE FLOTILLA tacked along lazily, as the admiral had no intention of venturing too near the islands until enemy airstrips had been properly pounded by the long-range bombers whose arrival from remote bases was delayed.

One day Dr. Hodges happened to be making his rounds aboard the *Daring*. When he finished, he strolled on deck with Clark and Bjorg, who continued to educate the lieutenant commander about the habits of cetaceans. They were watching the whale, of course, and noticed she was performing a new trick. She had come up close to the destroyer and was rubbing her head against its steel plates, while the powerful undulations of her tail kept her abreast of the ship.

"What the devil is she up to?" Clark asked, irritably. "Are these animals in the habit of rubbing themselves against ships?"

"They do it occasionally," Bjorg replied, "against

ships or floating wreckage they may happen on. What's she doing? Haven't you ever seen a flea-ridden dog rubbing up against a tree or a wall to dislodge the pests or at least relieve its itching? That's what our whale is doing. Instead of fleas, she has all kinds of more harmful parasites."

"Parasites?"

"The poor beast is covered with them; I've already noticed sea lice the size of hazelnuts, which all the pesticides on board won't kill. And that's just the beginning. Encrusted on these gigantic bodies are countless species of animal life. There are spiral-shaped *Coronulae,* barnacles that burrow under the skin; there are limpets and cirripeds, tiny and equally pernicious crustaceans. And the cruelest tormentor of all is the *Pennella,* which resembles a long black ribbon; it has horns and adheres like a snail. You can see them all over her head."

The whale's head was just below the three strollers. Bending forward, Clark discovered what looked like black worms clinging to the enormous mouth.

"These *Pennella* are vicious," Bjorg observed, continuing his lecture. "They attack where the skin is especially thin and sensitive. Our poor whale has collected hordes of them. These parasites have multiplied since we left South Georgia, for when whales are near the coast and ride above the waves, flocks of birds called phalaropes light on their backs and rid them of these pests. But here at sea there are no birds to perform this service. Look at her: there's a dark crust practically encasing her. She's lost that wonderfully magnetic blue color. See how she scratches her head against the hull. She must be in torment."

"That's all very well," Clark protested, unwilling to grieve over the matter, "but if she doesn't manage to ruin the plates, she'll surely damage the paint."

He ordered a sailor to take a broom and drive away this unwelcome, cheeky visitor, cautioning him to take care not to hurt her head. The sailor heard Bjorg's statement and knew just what to do. He went below and, through a porthole flush with the whale's mouth, poked at her with his broom.

Auntie Margot heeded the injunction and stopped scratching herself against the plates, but remained motionless, barely two feet away, as if waiting for the sailor to do something more. The sailor seemed puzzled. Sticking his head out the porthole, he looked up at Clark, who signaled him to push harder with the broom. The whale wouldn't budge and seemed to cast an imploring look out of its one visible, oddly situated eye. Suddenly, as if in response to the whale's plea, the sailor had an idea. With all his might he began to scrub the corners of her mouth that were crawling with tiny black eels: the *Pennella*. It was a stiff, heavy horsehair broom used for loosening dirt incrusted on the deck. It acted like a currycomb on the whale's skin, sending a host of dislodged parasites tumbling into the sea. Auntie Margot expressed her pleasure at this new lease on life by executing a joyful roll-over.

The sailor worked resolutely until he ran out of breath, which was all too soon because of his awkward stance with one arm outstretched. He could reach no more than a small patch of the colossal mouth, the left side of which was inaccessible, since the animal was on the port side. After brushing off the right corner of her mouth as best he could, he stopped and, taking his instructions from Clark, who stood watching above, again prodded the whale gently with his broom to persuade her that the grooming session was over—he could do no more for her and she had better clear out. Auntie Margot retreated a few yards and continued to swim alongside the ship on the port side. The look in her right eye, still fixed on the sailor with the broom, conveyed a mixture of gratitude and perplexity, as if she couldn't understand why such a successful operation had to end.

"She wants more. She's asking herself questions," Bjorg murmured pensively.

"Tell her to start thinking for herself," Clark grumbled, shrugging his shoulders.

Dr. Hodges, who had once studied the comparative psychology of animals and humans, said nothing, but appeared intensely interested in the whale's behavior. Like Bjorg, he was intrigued by her attitude and by the puzzled look in her eye, which seemed to reflect patient probing of a difficult problem perhaps beyond the mental capacity of a whale. She floated motionless, or nearly so; her spout, which previously shot up higher than the destroyer's deck, now rose feebly, as if she were holding her breath in order to concentrate on some herculean mental problem. Only the rhythmic, instinctive swaying of her tail kept her abreast of the vessel.

"I tell you she's asking herself questions, sir," Bjorg

insisted. "She's trying to solve her problem, and I'm ready to bet she'll do it."

"A bottle of whiskey says she doesn't," retorted Hodges. "But I wouldn't mind losing the wager," he muttered.

Irritated, Clark gave another sullen shrug but continued to observe the whale with growing curiosity and to find her behavior extraordinary. Her near-immobility lasted only a few minutes, then she seemed to come to life. In her eye, scarcely bigger than a human's, a spark flickered. Her breathing deepened; her tail swayed more rapidly. She left the destroyer's side and swam ahead, did a fast turnabout, and came back to the same side of the vessel facing the other direction, with her head presented at the porthole where the sailor still waited, holding his broom. With a quick prod he reached out for the other side of her mouth, which now was accessible.

"Won't solve a thing," murmured Hodges. "I'm about to win the bet."

"No, it won't," Bjorg agreed. "She'll have to do better than that, and she will, I'm sure. I'm doubling the bet, Doc."

"Two bottles if you like, on condition that you don't tamper with her."

"Agreed, Doc."

In fact, it was no solution to the problem. Whales were not created to swim backwards. Auntie Margot could only remain motionless, and in seconds the destroyer passed by, leaving her head beyond the sailor's reach. Crestfallen, he lowered his broom helplessly. The trio of watchers exchanged disappointed glances.

"I don't suppose you'd be willing to stop the ship for repairs, eh, Clark?" the doctor ventured.

Unappreciative of the joke, Clark shot him a fierce look and the three resumed their whale-watching. Auntie Margot did not try to repeat the maneuver but instead made another half-turn and took up her original position on the port side, swimming alongside the ship effortlessly, the same meditative look in her eye.

"It didn't take her long to discover her mistake," Bjorg commented. "She's trying to think up a better approach."

"Good Lord!" exclaimed Clark, "all she has to do..."

The three men exchanged knowing glances. The solution to the whale's problem had occurred to them at the same time and in their budding excitement they were eager to cue her on the right maneuver.

"All she really has to do..." Hodges repeated. "It's so simple."

"But she'll never find out," Clark groaned. "It's too much for the brain of a whale."

"That's why I made the bet," said the doctor.

"And I insist she will," Bjorg declared. "I'm going to win, Doc. Of course, it's a difficult and demanding problem for her, but cetaceans can solve many such problems. In the past, solitary sperm whales occasionally attacked the old whaling ships at their weakest point, which surely implies intelligence. As you've seen, sir, those savage killers, the orcas, are devilishly clever at rounding up their prey, and I don't have to tell you what patient training of dolphins can produce. Look at her: she's calculating, she's speculating."

By now all three had worked themselves up to such an excited pitch that every thought they uttered was inflated to epic proportions. Swept along by the former whaler's enthusiasm, the doctor declaimed lyrically:

"I do hope you're right, Bjorg! That means she must be examining her recent nonsuccess! Trial and error, frustrated efforts and lengthy meditation over her failures. Such sequences have led to the greatest scientific discoveries."

"How do you expect her to find out?" Clark protested. "She needs to be guided, to learn patterns of behavior, she needs patient training."

"She's coming to life now," Bjorg reported excitedly. "You say she won't find out, sir? Look at the gleam in her eye. She's stirring. She's going into action. She's ready to make another try."

For the second time the whale seemed to rouse herself from her apparent inertia. Slowly at first, then gaining momentum, as if eager to test the theory extracted from her meditation, she raced ahead of the destroyer just as she had done before. The three men eyed her anxiously, holding their breath, joined by crewmen who left their chores to watch, with throats strained, like agonized playgoers praying for a happy ending to a surprise-studded drama.

"She's about to repeat the same futile experiment," Clark moaned. "Look at her spurting ahead to make her turn. Stubborn persistence, just like an animal."

"Trial and error," Hodges repeated. "She is persistent, all right, but that's how scientific research operates. Einstein pursued all sorts of leads that dead-ended until he discovered the right track. This whale probably will have to make a good many errors before she succeeds."

"I suggest she's found the right track, Doc! She's not being obstinate like some foolish animal, as you put it, sir. Her thinking has paid off. She's changing directions, but not with a U-turn. She's no fool!"

It was true. Well ahead of the ship, the whale had simply angled off to the right, leaving the destroyer on her left and shifting to its starboard side.

"I've won the bet!" exclaimed the former whaler. "She solved the problem! We'll catch up with her when she slows down."

And the whale did just that.

"Sailor, cross over to starboard side!" the lieutenant commander shouted.

Needless command. Seeing the whale disappear behind the far side of the ship, the sailor with the broom had concluded that Auntie Margot was about to perform the very maneuver everyone hoped for. He dashed across the deck and stood waiting at a starboard porthole for the motionless whale as the ship caught up with her. The trio of observers was already above him. From all corners of the *Daring* rose a huge sigh of relief, along with scattered cheers when, as her head came abreast of the sailor, the whale began swimming rapidly enough to maintain that position, and more cheers went up when the man with the broom at last was able to dislodge the vermin fouling the left corner of her mouth.

"I lost my bet," declared Hodges, "and am I pleased!"

"We'll drink the whiskey together, Doc."

"I'm still not certain whether it's a manifestation of instinct, or if it's intelligence, as you propose. One would have to study the matter. In any event, I know a few human beings who wouldn't have solved the problem so fast."

The *Daring's* skipper said nothing, but his lips moved silently as if murmuring a prayer of thanks.

"Look at her eye," Bjorg said, "it's radiant."

True enough, the whale's left eye, which now watched them, seemed to glow with a strange light.

"*I triumph! I have stolen the Egyptians' secret of gold! I would surrender to my sacred ecstasy!*" recited the well-read doctor.

"What in heaven's name is all that about, Doc?" Clark asked, dumfounded.

"The proud words with which Kepler greeted his own discovery of planetary motion. The whale can't express herself in words, but if some of my colleagues could see her now, they'd admit that her elation rivals the rapture of that brilliant mathematician."

3

"NOW SHE'S rid of the worst of the *Pennella*," Bjorg declared once calm had returned to the destroyer, "but there are plenty of other parasites."

The three men had resumed their walk on deck. The broom-wielding sailor had cleaned off only the small patch as far as his arm would reach, and the whale had drifted off. Bjorg had an idea he continued to probe.

"Of course she can breathe more easily now, but that's only a palliative. Look, sir, that enormous body is encased in vermin and tiny crustaceans. It resembles the barnacle-ridden hull of a ship that's gone unscraped for years. Millions of tiny parasitic growths have attached themselves to her since we've been at sea. This crust not only irritates her skin but also hinders her movements and slows her down by preventing the water from sliding smoothly over her flanks—the same thing that happens to a ship."

"All right, but what can I do about it?" replied the lieutenant commander.

"Perhaps," Bjorg ventured, encouraged now to propose his idea, "perhaps a few more sailors could team up and work in crews all up and down the ship..."

"Out of the question," Clark snapped. "My men have more important duties than attending to the personal hygiene of your whale. To be effective, this kind of operation would take half my crew."

"I was thinking of the off-duty sailors."

"That's all I need! So they'll be worn out, with knees buckling when they come back on duty? I guessed what you were leading up to with your marvelous ideas, but I won't buy them. Out of the question. Do you know how much work that would take? A lot of hands doing a single chore."

Bjorg realized that the officer was right. Disappointed and dejected, he let the matter drop. But Hodges was in a pensive mood and pondered Clark's last words: a lot of hands doing a single chore.

As a result of his reflection, when Hodges returned to the admiral flagship he set about laying the psychological groundwork for the plan he had in mind. He held long telephone discussions with task force officers on board the transports. Hodges was popular with everyone at every level, and his advice always carried weight.

He had no trouble convincing them—since they knew it for a fact—that troop morale was deteriorating because there was nothing to do during the long voyage.

The whale's comings and goings had lessened the boredom to a certain extent, but what the men really needed was some kind of action. Their present idleness contrasted starkly with the vigorous training they had undergone and could not follow up on board. They were dying to land and would have welcomed any excuse for violent exercise that put their muscles to use. Having developed this theme with all the professional authority and friendly persuasion he could muster as a specialist in nervous disorders, the doctor proceeded casually to recount the whale's latest exploit, the outcome of which, alas, had been only mildly successful in thinning the hordes of her parasite invaders.

Sensing that they were psychologically prepared, Hodges sprang the idea he had conceived aboard the destroyer. It came as no great surprise to him that, instead of rejecting it, they found it altogether dazzling. As he talked, they began concocting similar programs of their own.

The seed was sown. The idea gained favor and, bit by bit, embellishment, as suggestions both practical and humanitarian were put forward, all to the credit of the army. Having thus won support from most of the commanding officers, it was presented next, along with a specific plan of action, to the army chief of staff by his senior officers and backed by the doctor's authority. As a result of these concerted efforts, the general reluctantly bowed to the eloquent logic of his advisers and, feeling disinclined to discuss such an extraordinary operation over the telephone, he headed for the flight deck after first requesting a conference with the admiral.

"If I understand you correctly," said the admiral, slightly puzzled by the general's fumbling approach to his subject, "you would like your troops to perform some special exercises to limber up their muscles and get them back into condition."

"That's more or less what I have in mind."

"How does that concern me, General? You can schedule any exercises you want as long as it doesn't interfere with the convoy's progress. It's not my business or my intention to become involved in a physical-fitness program for the land forces."

"No, of course not," the general replied with obvious embarrassment. "I just thought I'd check with you before setting up the program, since these exercises won't be strictly shipboard. I think the navy is also involved, and that's why I wanted to talk to you first."

"Not strictly shipboard?"

Taking a deep breath to bolster his courage, the general proceeded to outline the plan submitted to him, which he had rejected indignantly at the outset and finally come round to accept only under pressure from his staff: to bring the whale alongside the transports so that a few squads of soldiers could lower themselves on ropes to her level and scrape off the vermin disfiguring her coat.

The admiral frowned; this was not the first time it occurred to him that the blue whale was overrunning men's minds in the Royal Navy. Tempted to inquire whether the general was pulling his leg, he decided instead to add a healthy dash of acid to his response.

"Up to now, General, it was my impression that many of my officers were succumbing to a strain of contagious delirium induced by a whale. I was hoping—vainly, it seems—that the epidemic would confine itself to the navy; now, however, I note the army is also afflicted."

Still, he listened patiently to the arguments put forth by his visitor, who appeared undiscouraged by the chilly reception. Hodges had told him all about Auntie Margot's latest exploit and he too was impressed.

"I see no risk, Admiral. The sea is calm enough right now. My infantry, paratroops, and commandos are trained to fight under the worst conditions—even if they're dangling somewhere between heaven and earth."

"We're not talking about the earth," the admiral protested.

"The problem is not so different. I have a Gurkha platoon, you know. They're mountain folk, clever at clambering down cliffs at the end of a rope; this kind of exercise is right up their alley. If they can handle weapons at the same time, it should be a cinch for them to work with scrapers and currycombs that the shipboard workrooms have already begun turning out in quantity, excellent instruments, I'm told—and I've checked it out—for removing heavily incrusted parasites from the skin."

"Oh, the workrooms have already gone into production?"

"The Gurkhas had begun to whet their kukris, but

when they heard these might hurt the whale, they said they'd be willing to use the special tools."

The admiral interrupted him. "Isn't the kukri that dagger your Gurkhas use for slitting throats when they mop up enemy trenches—an operation for which they are particularly well suited?"

"That's right. It's the type of fighting they do best."

"How is it that these veteran warriors are prepared to do bath duty for a whale?"

"They can't wait to get started."

The two chiefs looked at each other in silence. The admiral appeared lost in thought.

"Go on," he said at last.

"As for the ropes we'll need, that won't present any problem since they're part of every commando's gear. We'll also need boards, which the carpenters can provide, plus a few other accessories."

"The same kind of mobile scaffolding they use to maintain public monuments?" the admiral growled, snapping out of his reverie.

The general nodded his head.

"All this at the mercy of a sudden ground swell that may fling your men into the sea and oblige my sailors to fish them out."

"They'll be safely attached—my officers will see to it—and at the first hint of foul weather we'll close down the operation. I've given strict orders on that account."

"I note you've already issued orders," the admiral commented with studied indifference.

"Instructions subject to your approval, Admiral.

That's the purpose of my visit. Of course, if you are firmly opposed, the project will be abandoned."

"That's great!" bellowed the admiral. "I'll look like a heartless monster, a pitiless executioner of men and beasts. How can I oppose it? After all, they're your soldiers. If there's a hitch, don't come running to me. It's your responsibility. Only..."

"Only?"

"I'll approve it, but I want you to know I think it's insane!"

The admiral calmed down and tried to reason with his caller.

"After all, General, didn't we come here—every soldier, sailor, petty officer, captain, and chief among us—to recapture the Falklands? It's a perilous undertaking that will demand our every effort. Men will be wounded, and some are bound to die. Before us lies a task for which we must be preparing constantly, which ought to fill our minds and occupy all our energies. Under these circumstances, don't you think it's utter madness to fool around with a whale that needs grooming? Good God!"

"I understand," the general replied, "but there's another way of looking at it. You spoke of the wounded and the dead: do you consider it humane, or even good practice, to deny innocent pleasure to men who are willing to lay down their lives in this expedition? I've studied the problem from all sides. My men are as gleeful as children to think they can comfort this whale. It's beyond my control. The whale now dwells in their minds. To deny them this pleasure would be a terrible disappointment, might even push them to the brink of despair. I've learned from experience that between hard-fought battles the stage is a great morale-booster for fighting men. In our situation we can't call in volunteer performers, but by sheer luck, Providence has sent our way..."

"A miraculous stroke of good fortune has sent this whale!" the admiral exploded. "Good God! I'll bet your soldiers have photographed Auntie Margot in every possible pose, that she's their latest pinup girl, after Marilyn and Raquel."

"It so happens that my officers have noted a few such exhibits," the general retorted coolly. "How did you guess?"

"My sailors have done the same thing! She's bewitched them. Well, go ahead, tidy up your whale, scratch her, pamper her, spruce her up till she gleams like a new penny on this gray ocean, like the Statue of Liberty lighting up the world. But I'm afraid your project will run aground."

"You foresee some problems, Admiral?"

"First of all, how will you manage to bring your transports alongside the whale? I'm not going to authorize any zigzag course for this convoy."

"No question of it. She's the one who will position herself alongside our ships. At least that's what everyone is hoping, and from what I gather as to the intelligence of this animal..."

"Intelligence!"

"That's the word they're using in every unit; you hear it from the officers, noncoms, and whale experts alike. Even Hodges goes along with it, though with certain reservations. So the consensus is that she will approach and present her back to the scrapers as soon as she sees the preparations we are making."

"Her back?" the admiral mused. "But I don't see how your plan will work. Your lascars are agile all right, and spectacularly good at dangling from a rope or clinging to a shaky scaffold, but they'll never be able to reach past the back of that colossus, maybe not even past a narrow strip along her flanks. I hope you're not expecting them to dive into this glacial sea."

"Not the paratroopers or the Gurkhas—though they'd do it willingly if ordered, mind you—it's not their specialty. This is a job for the frogmen, who are trained to work in icy waters and would relish the chance to dive under a whale's belly."

"I should have expected that," the admiral groaned. "You plan to muster up your frogmen too."

"I have several teams available, all volunteers, of course, and eager to get back into the water where they feel most at home. I think it would be an excellent training exercise for the missions we've planned for them later."

"I give up," the admiral announced, surrendering with a curt bow. "You've thought of everything. One word of advice, though. Do it fast; the briefest follies are the best. Right now we're in a peaceful zone, but once we come in range of enemy aircraft, there'll be no place for the kind of eccentric behavior you've just talked me into."

The general gave his word that, with the whale's cooperation, the operation would last no more than twenty-four hours at the limit. His staff had set up a tight schedule; to save time, the men would work as relay teams.

"Twenty-four hours," he declared. "The scrapers will scrape round the clock. Night duty will be excellent training for my men."

"Then I suppose you plan to use the searchlights?" the admiral protested.

"Never entered my head. My men don't need searchlights; they see perfectly well in the dark."

The admiral sighed and nodded resignedly.

4

THE NEXT day, when the whale was making her rounds of various units of the fleet, at a signal from observers aboard the lead troop transport who spotted her, the first wave of volunteers scrambled over the side onto ropes, calling her name, urging her to approach, and beckoning to her with their tools. At the same time a squad of frogmen in wetsuits took to the water, attached to long ropes reeled off the ship's prow that secured them without impeding their movements.

The general and his advisers were not disappointed. Instantly the whale grasped the significance of this scenario. Only for a second did she hesitate; then, with a series of graceful twisting, turning, rolling motions, came to rest against the side of the ship, her head at the prow and the tip of her tail nearly flush with the stern. The operation unfolded with the precision born of careful planning. Suspended astride their sawed-off planks resembling homemade swings, the soldiers went to work on the whale with unaccustomed zeal, rubbing, raking, scraping, brushing, balancing themselves from time to time with one or both feet on her broad back, which Auntie Margot tried her best to keep above the water line. The frogmen slipped under the leviathan's belly carrying more of the same tools, eager as the rest to do their job.

Working like demons in the cramped position they were forced to maintain, they could not possibly have continued beyond an hour or two. However, the general's staff had prepared a relay schedule for the various teams that gave every man aboard the transport a chance to share in the operation so that no one felt left out. Then the whale moved on to another ship where similar preparations had been made and the soldiers were waiting their turn impatiently. Thus, alternating between port and starboard, the clean-up job was completed in a day and a night, just as the general had promised.

Thanks to the efforts of all hands involved and to the marvels of organized British efficiency, the whale was rid of her parasites by dawn of the following day. Her skin sparkled like freshly waxed parquet; her handsome gray-blue coat, for which her species is named, was restored.

When the soldiers on the last transport had finished their job and climbed back up on deck, she withdrew majestically and prepared to thank all the crews in her fashion: a series of graceful undular plunges. The performance climaxed with the show-stopper she reserved for special occasions: a great vertical leap fueled by momentum gathered in the deep, propelling all one hundred fifty tons of her straight up out of the water, followed by a spectacular crashing dive that loosed a gigantic cascade of spray and a blast that shook the entire fleet.

"Look at her breaching after she just sounded," the admiral observed, for he too was succumbing to whalers' jargon.

The general arrived to report the success of the operation, and both men contemplated Auntie Margot's rolling motions as they stood on the carrier's deck. The admiral had let slip a cry of admiration during the whale's gala performance. This made him thoughtful, and prompted a monologue which, on his lips, sounded very strange.

"Sometimes I wonder where this animal comes from and what exactly she is. Such contagious infatuation is unnatural; first it swept the officers and crew of the *Daring*, then gradually overcame all units of the fleet, your soldiers, and finally you, General. Maybe we're sailing an enchanted ocean fraught with magic spells. Maybe our ancestors back in the Dark Ages were right to believe that witches or demons appeared in the form of animals. They saw evil spirits in a cat or a werewolf. Why not a whale? Was Auntie Margot sent from heaven or hell? God created a huge fish for the sole purpose, it seems, of swallowing Jonah to punish him for his sins and then coughing him up after he had suffered suitably. I must talk to the padre about this."

Snapping out of his reverie, he gave the general a friendly slap on the shoulder and reverted to his usual manner.

"Just between the two of us, General, man to man, forget for a moment that we're in charge of this expedition and answer me frankly. Do you think any other army and navy anywhere in the world would behave as insanely as we have over a whale?"

"Frankly, no," the general replied, smiling.

"Neither do I. I know something about the American navy and feel sure they would have avoided many of these problems. At the first radar signal they might have been tempted to pump a bellyful of lead into Auntie Margot."

"And a great shame it would have been, for she's really a beautiful animal," the general concluded. "After all, perhaps it's no crime to be a bit eccentric."

Her performance over, the blue whale settled down, relaxed her pace, and paraded past the fleet one last time in her stunning new finery, rolling over to display a glistening gray-blue and black mottled belly studded with her newly recovered white spots.

She stretched her visit nearly to a half hour, then returned to her self-designated post as ship's scout just ahead of the destroyer *Daring*.

5

Back in London, Betsy and Joan, two young women attached to the military censor's office, began opening letters from the Falklands task force. A fast ship had carried the mail to South Georgia, where it was put aboard a plane bound for the British capital. Betsy, the elder, was a captain; Joan, a lieutenant.

To their astonishment, the current stack of letters was all about an animal. Unlike previous batches complaining about the long, tedious voyage or reflecting the aggressive tensions of seasoned fighting men, these letters revealed a single and very different theme: the blue whale.

"Listen to this, Joan," said Betsy, adjusting her glasses. "I'm just picking one at random. I could tell you straight off what this chap is going to say."

She read aloud from a paratrooper's letter describing in great detail how his commando outfit had spent hours scraping Auntie Margot's back and was rewarded by her with a show of sensational dancing.

"Auntie Margot," Joan interrupted, musing. "Maybe it's a secret password."

"It's a whale. You can tell from what follows."

"The ones I've got are also about a whale," Joan continued. "Mostly from the destroyer *Daring*. Yes, that's it, the men named her Auntie Margot. All the letters go on and on about her; some are really astounding. Take this one, for instance. It's from a petty officer on the *Daring* to his girl friend, I suppose. Listen:

"'You can't imagine how affectionate this whale is, sweetie, and how attached to us she's become. She gets friendlier every day and is just as obedient as your dog Inkspot. Mr. Bjorg, who's studied the habits of whales and knows more about them than all the academic experts put together—he's also taught dolphins some amazing stunts back home—Mr. Bjorg has managed to communicate with Auntie Margot using what he calls a silent whistle. Silent, because we can't hear it; but the whale hears it, amazing thing. Yesterday, when some sailors and I were off duty—I got the O.K. from Mr. Clark, our skipper and a swell guy—Mr. Bjorg gave a demonstration of just how cooperative, intelligent, and obedient this animal is. We were sitting on deck in a circle around the whaler and he asked each of us in turn:

"'Do you want her to approach the ship, John, or move away?'"

"'Do you want her to shift from port to starboard side, George?'

"'Would you like her to stay still, Lou, and let the *Daring* pass by?'

"After each question, and according to the man's answer, Mr. Bjorg would click his tongue into what looks like a whistle. As I say, we couldn't hear a sound, but Auntie Margot acted on the command. It was unbelievable; we were stunned. Lou, the fat fellow whose family believes in ghosts, mumbled something about witchcraft. I don't go for witches or elves, but it reminds me of clairvoyance sessions in which a man questions a blindfolded woman who is able to 'read' the letters and numbers on identity papers in the wallet of someone in the audience chosen at random. But the best part came when Mr. Clark—a swell guy, as I said, career officer but not too snotty to talk when we're off duty—when Mr. Clark was on deck and stopped to talk to Mr. Bjorg:

"'Ask her to swim in a circle around the destroyer.'"

"'I'm not sure she'll be able to do it,'" Mr. Bjorg replied with a smile. "'Her education has just begun; but I can always try.'"

"'Which he did with more clicking and smacking noises into the silent whistle. We held our breath. Well, guess what, sweetie, it worked! Auntie Margot made a large circle around us. Of course she halted and hesitated and wandered off a couple of times, until Mr. Bjorg signaled her back onto the right track. She ended up exactly where she started. Isn't that astounding?' . . . What do you think, Betsy?"

"Astounding!" Betsy grumbled, frowning. "What really astounds me, though, is that none of these chaps gives the slightest thought to parents or friends who are worried sick for their safe return. They're obsessed with this whale. Listen, Joan, here's what the chief cook on that same destroyer writes:

"'Auntie Margot seems friendlier every day, so I wanted to thank her for coming around regularly and giving us a good show. It isn't easy, though. I thought I'd toss her a goody next time she swims up close, and she often does. At first I figured the kitchen smells were attracting her, but it isn't that. She doesn't come begging for bones like a dog. Mr. Bjorg, who knows more about these whales than anyone, told me she hears everything even with ears so small you can hardly see the opening, but she has a rotten sense of smell. So I asked myself what kind of food would appeal to such a huge body and was about to throw her an extra haunch of meat out of my locker. Mr. Bjorg was there and stopped me in time. The blue whale, he told me, has a very narrow gullet and feeds only on plankton—microscopic particles drifting in the water—or krill. A leg of lamb would never go down. How about a lump of sugar? I asked him. Not even powdered sugar, he warned me, saying that Auntie Margot and all her relatives are used to a very salty diet and any change in her eating habits could make her sick.

"'So I took a few packages of the saltines we give the boys with their beer and I grated them very fine— Mr. Bjorg thought about it and decided it couldn't do her any harm. I spread a layer of this powder on the water when she swam up to the ship and was happy to watch her gulp it down—mixed with a bunch of plankton, I'm sure. Such a small gift for a giant, but that's the best I can manage.' What do you say to that, Joan?"

"Bless them all! It's very touching."

"Touching?" Betsy scoffed. "If you ask me, they're all losing their marbles. This whale has them mesmerized. Not a word about how they are or if the weather's calm or stormy. No mention of when they expect the fighting to start."

"Everyone seems spellbound, including the officers," Joan commented. "Here's what the captain of the *Daring* writes to his wife."

Betsy listened, frowning steadily, while Joan was inclined to be sympathetic. The lieutenant commander poured out a raptuous account of how the whale had tried and failed, then put her mind to the problem and was smart enough to shift over to the starboard side in order to present the left corner of her mouth for cleaning. Joan read his parting comments on the scene.

"'Ridiculous as it may seem, dear, I must admit that in the short space of time between her failed attempt, her deliberation, and her ultimate success, I was a bundle of nerves. I felt torn by hope and despair—the way I felt when our little Mary was crawling around on all fours and struggled to her feet one day, collapsed, and pulled herself upright again to take her first triumphant step...' What do you say to that, Betsy?"

"It's not the way most naval officers talk. I still think they're all candidates for the loony bin; I'll bet there's something strange going on aboard that ship."

"Here's a letter from the fellow named Bjorg they've mentioned a few times. It's addressed to his son, who lives here somewhere on the coast. This is what he writes:

"'... As she showed such promise, I thought it would

be possible to educate this animal and develop her intelligence as we've done with the dolphins. What's more, I'm about to succeed. You must admit it was far more difficult. Auntie Margot wasn't always close by, nor could I reward her with a tidbit, which is fundamental to the learning process. But all along I had the impression I was dealing with an exceptional subject and kept imagining ways to communicate with her. You know how sensitive marine animals are to ultrasonic vibrations—like dogs, only much more so, as I've found out. If this whale and her mate didn't react immediately to the asdic beam, it may have been because they weren't alarmed; they did react, however, after a delay, even at great depths. I discovered in my luggage one of those silent whistles that emit such vibrations; we use them to train dogs and also in our dolphin experiments. I tried it out on Auntie Margot, with encouraging results. In a very short time I was able to set up a kind of code that no other creature could have understood. Depending on the length and intensity of the vibration, she approached or moved away. She also swims straight ahead and turns right or left on command. If she makes a mistake, a long series of rapid vibrations is all it takes to point out the error and set her back on course. If we had the time, I'm sure I'd have her performing even more brilliantly than our dolphins...' No use reading any further, Betsy. This only bears out and explains what the petty officer was saying, which sounded pretty far out."

"Maybe they're both nuts," Betsy muttered.

"I don't see how we can censor this mail," said Joan, a newcomer to the job. "There are no military secrets."

"I suppose there aren't, but it's all so odd that I think we should show it to the boss."

Which she did. The colonel in charge threw up his hands and admitted he couldn't figure out what was going on in the heads of the letter-writers. After some discussion, though, he agreed that the contents did not require censoring but cautioned the young women to pay special attention to the rest of the mail and to subsequent batches that were expected shortly. He wanted a full report, with samples of the juiciest passages. If they turned out to be as heady as the last lot, he would decide whether or not to inform the higher-ups of the alarming mental attitude rampant in the Falklands task force.

It was a big job, involving thousands of letters. Betsy and Joan set to work, Betsy pouting sullenly at every snatch of purple prose, Joan, the neophyte, smiling at each marvelous adventure of Auntie Margot.

6

THE FLEET was approaching the islands and the fringes
of the danger zone. All units were on permanent alert,
although no planes had been sighted. It was overcast
much of the time, a thick blanket of fog having settled
in the atmosphere, making air attacks virtually impossible. A frigid rain fell constantly, mixed at times with
snow flurries. The seamen had put on cold-weather gear
under their oilskins. The blue whale continued to lead
the convoy and seemed unperturbed by the rigors of the
weather.

One morning the captain of the *Daring* was called
to the bridge by the watch officer, who reported sighting
a strange object in the water.

"The whale drew my attention, sir; she seems to be
playing with it. Flotsam, I suppose; funny looking,
though. It was hard to see anything in this fog, but now
it's lifting. Over there, less than a quarter of a mile."

They both peered through binoculars. Sure enough, the whale was behaving oddly. With her enormous head she was pushing and prodding an object that, in size and shape, resembled a barrel. Clark replied to a suggestion from the watch officer:

"That's no barrel, or else it floated in from somewhere else. I've now forbidden the men to toss barrels to her. Nobody would be foolish enough to disobey my orders. I think it's clearly understood that this is not an amusement park."

A few days earlier the sailors had entertained themselves by pitching some empty barrels to the whale and watching her chase them about. But this kind of horseplay ended when the fleet approached the danger zone. Still, the unknown object looked cylindrical, and Auntie Margot was giving it her barrel treatment. All but totally immersed, its shape was hard to discern from the bridge until she butted it and sent it bouncing over the waves as if in a game of water polo. The fog was breaking up, though cottony sheets of it still hung in the air, churned by the wind and reducing the visibility. During one bright interval that lasted longer than most, the mysterious object emerged more clearly when the whale poked it above the waves. Clark went white and shouted:

"My God, it's a mine! And she's banging on it like a punching bag!"

He fired off a series of commands, ordering the ship to heave to. All guns were trained on the mine and, of necessity, on the whale, who seemed to enjoy her sport. She and her plaything frolicked at a few hundred yards from the ship. Clark was about to signal for the gunners to open fire and set off the mine when a flood of guilt changed his mind.

"Get Bjorg over here, quick!"

Bjorg arrived seconds later; his practiced eye needed no binoculars to size up the situation. Hastily the lieutenant commander briefed him on the crisis, which he had instantly perceived.

"A mine—not a contact mine, which would have gone off by now thanks to the bumping around it got from your blessed whale. This type of weapon is designed to withstand impact and to explode only on exposure to a magnetic field such as any large ship produces. I'll explain it later. The point is that if the mine gets much closer, we'll all be pulverized. I've ordered the gunners to fire if it invades a given safety zone. And your whale is delivering it right to our doorstep as if she wanted to entertain us."

"She probably does," Bjorg observed calmly.

"If she comes within a hundred—no, a hundred and fifty—yards, I shall have to blow up that blasted mine."

"You'll blow up Auntie Margot too."

"I can't help it."

"You forget the favor she did you by locating the mine."

"I can't help it," Clark repeated coldly.

"A hundred and fifty yards, you said, sir? That's about as far as my signals to her can reach. She's almost there. Give me a minute."

"Thirty seconds, that's all," the captain shot back, looking at his watch.

Bjorg put the silent whistle to his lips and began to

produce vibrations inaudible to the human ear. At first the whale paid no attention and kept up the lethal game that brought her closer and closer to the ship. Studying his watch, Clark had raised his arm to indicate that time was running out.

"Wait, sir," Bjorg pleaded, "I think I've got it."

Suddenly the whale stopped playing. Nearly motionless now, she was edging up to the safety zone set by the captain. Clark lowered his arm slowly and mopped his brow.

Bjorg continued sending his messages. Auntie Margot waited impatiently, as if annoyed at having her fun disrupted; then, seemingly resigned, she reluctantly swam away from the mine. Clark and all the crewmen heaved a sigh of relief.

The lieutenant commander waited for the whale to distance herself from the explosive, then ordered his gunners to blast it out of the water. The second shell hit its mark: the lethal device detonated in a towering geyser of foam. Anyone observing the whale at that moment was impressed by her reaction. Immobile, her head partly submerged and facing the pyrotechnic display, she seemed just as perplexed as she had been when confronted earlier with the problem of cleaning the corners of her mouth.

"She's saved us, sir," said Bjorg. "In this fog, if she hadn't been there, you never would have spotted that half-hidden mine. The destroyer was heading straight for it. And you were going to kill her!"

"I would have done it, too—regretfully. Of course,

I'm glad it happened this way, but actually, we might not have been hit. Like most naval units, the *Daring* is equipped with an electrical device to reduce its magnetic field for just this purpose. It's not foolproof though, and I wouldn't have risked our necks."

Meanwhile, the high command had dispatched two patrol boats used to hunt and destroy mines. Forever curious about nautical matters, Bjorg wanted to know how they operated. While the boats were maneuvering, Clark explained that each trailed an electric cable of a different length that carried an electrode at the tip. The resulting magnetic field was strong enough to set off any explosive device located between the two electrodes within a fairly wide radius.

"I doubt if there's a mine field here," he added. "We're still too far from the islands. This one probably was laid near the coast and floated out on the current. So there might be others around too."

While Clark was explaining all this, both men had more or less forgotten about the whale. She hadn't budged since the explosion and continued to look thoughtful. The active patrol boats seemed to spark her keen interest.

"The blast didn't scare her," Clark observed.

"She felt she had escaped a menace," Bjorg declared, "and by the same token had saved us from one."

"What's she doing now? She seems to be stirring and swimming off."

"She's on her own now, sir," Bjorg exclaimed, always bursting with excitement whenever the whale acted independently. "My sonar can't reach her anymore. I predict that she understood what happened and will behave accordingly."

The whale made off at a clip, on a serpentine course not unlike that of the patrol boats, weaving back and forth, exploring every inch of ocean.

"A bird dog on the scent," Bjorg commented; "her head is submerged because she sees better under water than above it, and in her own element she relies on other mysterious senses more subtle than sight. She's taken on the same mission as your patrol boats; her senses function like their electrodes. She's making sure to keep out of their way; while they cover the starboard side, she operates off the port side. I'll bet she's scouring the waves as thoroughly as your fellows."

"You're probably right," murmured Clark, beginning to share the former whaler's utter confidence in Auntie Margot.

"There, what did I tell you!" exclaimed Bjorg exultantly. "She's flushed another quarry, a second mine, sir! And what does she do next? Does she poke and prod it like a beach ball? Nothing of the sort. She's not stupid. She's learned that this is not a game. She nudges it as gently as that monstrous body of hers can manage in a choppy sea."

Auntie Margot was doing exactly that. After admiring this awesome performance, Clark felt the familiar stirrings of anxiety.

"But she's pushing the mine toward us," he cried in alarm.

"Of course. She's still far away, but she's coming nearer. Can't you see what she's up to?"

"I see that if she gets too close, favor or no favor, I'll have to blow her up. Send her that message, Bjorg. Tell her to keep her distance."

"She's still beyond my range, sir; anyway, there's no point. She won't come close to the ship. I don't have to tell her that. Her every move is designed to bring the prey—an enemy of sorts, like a killer whale, which is a threat only to us—in range of your guns so that you can send it to join the orcas. When she's done that, she'll move off voluntarily, head for the open sea, and leave you free to destroy the foe. Sorry, sir, but I don't intend to obey you. I won't send her any instructions... Wait, what did I tell you? Auntie Margot has completed her mission. She's taking cover."

Slowly and deliberately he put the useless whistle back in his pocket. Once again he had sized up the situation accurately: after giving the mine one last nudge for good measure, the whale turned and swam off hurriedly, to wait and watch a hundred yards or so from the ship.

She didn't have to wait long. A single shell sufficed to set off the mine. Another explosion reverberated like an echo as a third mine succumbed to the flawless technique of the patrol boats. Then the motorized hunters and the whale resumed their minestalking, each in his own manner, with different but equally effective weapons. No other mines turned up that day.

"I'm so grateful to have seen this miracle with my

own eyes!" Clark murmured. "Bjorg, your whale is a marvel."

"She's improving all the time, sir. I'll make one more prediction: the day will come when she won't need to receive instructions."

7

WAR BROKE out on the sea and in the air. The fleet
was deployed off Soledad, the larger of the two Falklands.
Port Stanley's airfield had been badly damaged by heavy
bombers from remote bases. A second airstrip located
on a smaller island had been crippled by a frogman commando unit. But long-range bombers dispatched from
the Argentine coast were making frequent sorties and
harassing the British armada. Swooping in, the planes
had to release their bombs, reverse, and head back to
faraway home bases in a matter of minutes. The destruc-
tiveness of these raids did credit to the bold determination of crack pilots risking their necks to forestall a
landing generally considered imminent, and challenging
the British navy's daily bombardment of Soledad's stra-
tegic targets. Several warships had been heavily damaged; two sank. Among the seamen, casualties were
mounting, some dead, many more wounded; enemy pi-

lots fared likewise. In this wartime climate nobody paid much attention to the whale.

Contrary to the admiral's prediction, the whale did not run for cover when bombs and shells began to burst. She kept up her rounds of the fleet, only more cautiously and in a different mood. Surprised at first by the infernal man-made din visited on that normally peaceful region, where an occasional blustery gale or the cries of a seal herd pursued by orcas produced the loudest noise, the whale seemed to have grown used to it. Bjorg claimed she had *adapted* to a state of war, and Dr. Hodges was inclined to agree.

Like urban populations at the sirens' warning, the blue whale had developed a habit of diving for cover in an air raid. She did it in her own fashion—which was nothing to scoff at—by sounding deep at the approach of warplanes. Down below, with two or three hundred feet of water to protect her, she was safer than in a concrete bunker. She took the warning not from sirens but from her own highly tuned hearing circuitry capable of distinguishing the engine sounds of friendly ships from those of hostile planes, and perhaps also from other mysterious senses unknown to humans, as Bjorg maintained. Thus her own early-warning system operated more effectively than radar, which was partly blinded by high waves and by the Argentine pilots' practice of approaching low over the water.

She would linger near the ocean floor, holding her breath as long as possible. By the time she surfaced for air, the alert usually was ended. If not, if a second wave of planes had arrived and bombs were still falling, she would arch her great back, rapidly expel the three to four cubic meters of foul air trapped in her lungs, greedily inhale a like quantity of fresh air, and plunge back down to her underwater refuge from man's destructive folly.

When at last she reappeared and found the skies clear after enemy planes had headed home, except for the ones whose smoking wreckage littered the ocean, the whale contemplated this destruction with surprise and chagrin. It made her especially sad to see black smoke curling from hard-hit units of the fleet. She would twist her way through the debris, nosing it anxiously the way survivors of an air raid gingerly pick through the rubble of city streets, half afraid they may unearth the corpse of a loved one. Instinct always brought her back to the *Daring,* and once she had determined that it was safe and no mournful plume of smoke issued from the destroyer's flanks, Auntie Margot broke into one of her choreographic fantasies in joyful celebration.

So far the destroyer had escaped serious damage. Pure luck. A bomb had pierced the bridge and lodged near a magazine. Fortunately, it was dismantled before it exploded. Only a few sailors were wounded when it struck. Clark thanked his stars for this lucky break, while certain less sophisticated crewmen credited the miracle to their protector and mascot, Auntie Margot.

Afterward, the blue whale was left pretty much to her own devices. Bjorg, her mahout, as Clark dubbed him teasingly, had been transferred to one of the troop transports cruising on the edge of the battle zone and secretly preparing to make a landing west of the larger island (not where the Argentines expected it), shielded by naval artillery they were relying on for protection against air attack. The high command felt that Bjorg, with his expert knowledge of the terrain, was just the man to lead the landing spearhead.

At first the whale felt disappointed to hear no more signals from the silent whistle. She seemed a bit nervous and circled the *Daring*, butting against the hull. At last she came to terms with the situation, or so it appeared, for she settled down. As the former whaler declared on leaving the destroyer, she had matured enough to manage her own life.

8

"WELL, here's something different," said Betsy impatiently, tipping back in her chair opposite Joan's and adjusting the glasses she relied on to help decipher some of the less exemplary specimens of penmanship. "This letter is not from the ordinary crewman, or a petty officer, or even a lieutenant commander. It's from a colonel, a doctor who specializes in treating mental illness— he must be pretty smart to begin with, judging from the big words he uses. He's writing to a doctor friend of his attached to a university. Well, he starts out talking about the men's frame of mind—naturally, since that's his specialty—but the rest is all about the whale's mind."

"That whale again," Joan murmured.

"Again and forever. If the academics are losing their grip, then we're in for trouble."

"There are others, you know, besides sailors, soldiers, and academics," observed Joan. "Here's a letter from a protestant chaplain to another minister. Same one-track mind."

After examining the first mail delivery, the two young women in the censor's office had received a second, equally large batch sent off just after the *Daring*'s encounter with the magnetic mines. Nothing surprised them anymore about the writing they were called on to scrutinize. Betsy shrugged impatiently; Joan admitted that the letters were fun to read, like a thriller. One and the same subject seemed to preoccupy every writer: the blue whale. Earlier correspondence had described each step of Auntie Margot's grooming, with all the soldiers participating. This latest mail waxed rhapsodic over the current idol's remarkable feat of detecting the magnetic mines and shepherding them within firing range. The epistolary styles varied: some revealed a near-mystical state of exaltation; others took Auntie Margot for a benevolent spirit or else a witch in a whale's disguise; still others worshipped her outright, presaging the birth of a new religious cult.

In this respect the letter from a Gurkha corporal to his family in Nepal was rather informative. After reciting the whale's singular accomplishments, he wrote:

"Night and day, time passes slowly and I ask myself questions. We all know that God is reincarnated periodically on Earth in order to combat evil and restore justice. When it comes to our whale, I can't help thinking of the ten avatars of Vishnu the Preserver. As you know, these include several animals: a tortoise, a boar, a monster half-man half-lion, destined to strike down Hiranyaka-sipu, faithless worshipper of Shiva the Destroyer. Vishnu's subsequent incarnations were human: a dwarf; the first Rama; then a second Rama, son of Jamadagni; Krishna, and finally Buddha. Of all these incarnations, dear parents, I have neglected to mention the most impressive: the initial one, the *matse-avatar*. He can be seen in the famous Grotto of Elephanta, a small island off the coast of Bombay where you took me on a pilgrimage when I was a child. The grotto—actually a man-made cave—is very ancient. It goes back seven centuries before Christ, according to Western tradition. Vishnu the Preserver is represented as a man from the waist up; below the waist is something resembling a large fish, which people nowadays take for an awkwardly drawn whale. Surely Vishnu's first incarnation was a whale. If you've been counting, that makes only nine avatars; the tenth, as we all know, has yet to happen and we await it. Certain gurus, called prophets in this part of the world, have already named him Kalki and identified him as a white-winged horse of evil intent—I don't know why—bent on destroying the universe, an idea that conflicts with everything we ever learned about our loving God. Incredible! Since coming here—and don't blame me for it, dear parents—I have decided to take gurus and prophets with a grain of salt.

"We await fervently this tenth avatar of Vishnu. I should say we were awaiting it, for I have no doubt that it has occurred. The miracle has come to pass. The Preserver is reincarnated just as the ancient gurus foresaw—and they carry more weight than the current crop—but for his final terrestrial appearance he chose to repeat his earliest one, thus providing an excellent demonstration of divine harmony. This is the truth as I have seen it in sleepless nights of meditation and prayer: the last reincarnation of Vishnu is a whale, our blue whale, which the British (for reasons I cannot discover) have named Auntie Margot and which has come to protect mankind rather than destroy it. We soldiers of the Falklands expeditionary force are the first to enjoy these blessings, and I have been honored to cleanse the back of our God."

"The chaplain's letter and the Gurkha corporal's have something in common," Joan observed. "Their beliefs differ, but both suggest a supernatural side to this whale. Listen, Betsy:

"'I have spent the night pondering the nature of this whale...'"

"Starts out the same way," Betsy commented.

"True. '...and I re-read more carefully chapter 41 of Job, Isaiah 27 and Psalm 104, where the leviathan is described. Well, I'm now convinced that the dreadful monster cannot be a whale, no matter what some people say. This smacks of a misleading and dangerous interpretation of the Old Testament that I will do my best to combat when I return to England. Can you imagine? The dragon that the Lord would smite with his terrible sword is supposed to be a harmless cetacean? And here's another one that, as I recall, says: "His body is like unto breastplates of molten bronze and covered with scales that stick together as with a closed seal"? That scarcely resembles the skin of our whale, which is smooth and lovely in color. A repulsive, terrifying monster? Come now! And the moral perspective is even more wobbly. "A heart firm as stone"? Why, our whale is the essence of sensitivity and kindness. The devil incarnate, others say? I'd raise the roof if anger weren't a sin. Why, she's the very essence of virtue, an angel: that's how she strikes me.' No point reading any further, Betsy. He goes on to cite more passages from the Bible, this time in Latin sprinkled with some Hebrew words. The gist of it is that he too has only one thing on his mind: the whale."

"That goes for the neurologist, Joan. I'm skipping the beginning of his letter where he speaks of certain neuroses diagnosed among the soldiers. He doesn't go into much detail. Now, listen to what he says to his doctor friend:

"'I know you've done a good deal of study and research in comparative psychology, which attempts to compare mental faculties of humans and animals as well as certain man-eating plants. Too bad you didn't join this Falklands expedition, as we have a subject that would catch your fancy. It's a whale, but no ordinary one.'"

"Here we go again. I should have known," Joan interrupted.

"We'll never hear the end of it. I'm skipping his description of the animal, its size, color, and marvelous accomplishments. We've been through that already. Then he goes on: 'I've spent entire nights trying to understand what makes this animal tick.'"

"So has the chaplain."

"The Gurkha corporal too, along with every soldier

and sailor. They all lie awake nights dreaming of a whale. It's weird, Joan."

"Perhaps," Joan replied mysteriously, "perhaps we ought to be more indulgent and take into account the conditions under which these fellows have been living for a month, off in the middle of nowhere, no girl friends in sight."

"I guess you mean they're sexually frustrated," Betsy declared judicially.

"Something like that," Joan replied, blushing.

"According to his letter, the doctor is about to retire. Listen to the rest of this instead of making foolish guesses.

"'With respect to this whale's behavior, I have given a good deal of thought to C. Lloyd Morgan's statement, which you know as well as I do: *In no case may we interpret an action as the outcome of the exercise of a higher psychical faculty if it can be interpreted as the exercise of one which stands lower in the psychological scale*. Aside from the style of writing, which I don't much favor, I'm sure you agree that the statement itself is open to debate. But I'll accept it as a working premise. This premise would lead us to believe that the Venus's-flytrap, for instance, which snaps shut the moment an insect lights upon it, acts instinctively from a need for food; or that a mollusk does the same by closing its shell at the approach of its hereditary foe, the starfish. One could safely rule out rational behavior and call it simply a physical adaptation to given conditions. But to come back to the whale, after analyzing her performance on the occasions I described to you, I'm tempted to conclude that the exercise of a relatively high psychical faculty is involved, to use Morgan's words, since I cannot see any faculty lower on the scale that could cause such behavior. This is all hypothetical, of course. Or maybe I'm indulging in anthropomorphism by attributing human feelings to a whale. What do you think? . . . ' And it goes on from there, Joan, giving a bunch of examples of animal behavior and mentioning weird names I've never heard of."

"Know what I think? They're all half dotty, that Falklands task force. . . . Now, this should complete the file for the boss to see. I'll take it right in to him."

The colonel in charge of military censorship examined the file that Betsy brought. He too was nonplused, found it most irregular, and determined to alert the higher-ups to this extravagant emotional outpouring from the brave lads gone off to recapture some remote islands.

9

THE SHIP Bjorg had boarded was cruising with other troop transports at some distance from the straits separating the two principal islands, East Falkland and West Falkland. A number of light units had landed successfully the night before on the eastern one, renamed Soledad Island, in the Bay of San Carlos, and had established a beachhead there in order to move the main army and heavy reinforcements to the island the following night. Bjorg was part of this second contingent, which had stayed clear of the projected landing site during the day while most of the fleet, positioned in the straits, shielded the commandos ashore from enemy air attack.

Late in the afternoon these reinforcements started on their way to San Carlos. Bombing raids throughout the day had done some damage to the fleet, but not enough to halt the consolidation and enlargement of the beachhead. The rest of the operation was expected to progress on schedule. Night was falling, and a low cloud cover minimized the threat of further air assaults until the next morning.

Though not part of the fighting force, Bjorg was as eager to go ashore as the armed and equipped combat troops. Beyond the lure of this adventure lay his deep attachment to the land that had taught him his sailing and whaling skills, both from firsthand experience on those stormy seas and from the epic tales of real harpooners like his grandfather. As the fleet neared the island, he saw through a break in the clouds the rugged coastal cliffs outlined against a dusky evening sky.

Just at that moment all hell broke loose. Unseen and unheralded, a squadron of planes appeared out of nowhere, zooming over the waves in what seemed to be a favorite tactic of the Argentine pilots, and attacked the transports. Antiaircraft guns opened up; carrier-based fighters took to the air, too late to halt the destruction. Several ships were hit and one of the transports, the very one to which Bjorg had transferred, found itself squarely in the path of a torpedo.

An explosion outdeafening all the others attested to the ship's doom. The men nearest the torpedo's point of impact were instantly blown to bits. Others were hurled overboard, stunned out of their senses, and drowned. The lucky few who stood clear of the devastating blast stripped off their gear and leaped into the sea, for the flooded ship was sinking fast, taking with it any unfortunate souls unable to free themselves in time.

Bjorg was among the survivors. He found himself alone, at some distance from the sinking ship, unclear as to how his instincts had pushed him that far. He wasn't much better off being alive, though, for the water was like ice. He had managed to grab hold of an empty crate floating nearby, but realized there was little chance of holding out against the creeping numbness overcoming his limbs.

By now the attack planes had left the scene. Rescue efforts were under way in a climate of general panic. The warships had all they could do to look after their own casualties and repair their own damage. A thick fog hung over the water, making it impossible to send up helicopters. Semidarkness hampered the search attempts of a destroyer escort and several corvettes, all virtually unscathed, that had approached the stricken ship while the remainder of the convoy continued on toward the coast. When night finally fell, the rescue ships ran the added risk of colliding with one another and had little hope of locating survivors. A few dinghies had been lowered into the choppy waters, but they too groped about aimlessly in the dark.

Bjorg gradually was becoming chilled to the bone; he could barely cling to his improvised buoy. He felt desperately alone, which merely reinforced the grim prospect of impending, inescapable death. Still, others must be suffering the same agony. The transport had been packed with troops; not all of them could have perished. He sensed that it would comfort him to make contact with other survivors and would help him to struggle a little longer against the icy tide invading his body. He had tried to cry out, but his voice was too faint to challenge the churning waters.

Just as he was getting used to the idea of dying—even of letting himself drown to cut short the agony—he heard a ship's siren. Half-delirious, he felt certain it belonged to the destroyer *Daring*, his home for several weeks and the source of many friends. The sound revived his courage. He flexed his muscles, gone nearly rigid from the cold, and with hope in his heart, listened.

No, it wasn't a dream. He hadn't slipped into a coma. It was a real siren. Not surprising either in the pea-soup fog. But there was no way to tell how far off it was. Once again he tried to shout, to stretch his arm above the water and wave. Crazy. No sound came forth, and his feeble gesture was lost in the night. For his pains, all he got was a mouthful of oil-saturated brine.

The siren sounded near at times, then far away. The ship must be on an irregular serpentine course. Maybe there were other, luckier castaways who had been picked up. Yes, it was all a matter of luck. And luck doesn't accept help.

His panic abruptly turned to violent rage at the thought of his helplessness. He beat his chest in despair and frustration, which only made him dunk his head and swallow another brackish mouthful. But drowning no longer tempted him. Struggling to keep his mind alert against the creeping numbness, he tried to think of a way to signal rescuers.

Suddenly an idea flashed through his mind as he fought desperately against the mental paralysis gradually overtaking him; actually, it was only the kernel of an idea trying to take shape and not succeeding, despite the best efforts of his impaired senses. Strange and absurd as it seemed in his condition, he found himself recalling a passage he had memorized from one of his favorite authors. It was Edgar Allan Poe describing the impressions of his tormented hero in "The Pit and the Pendulum":

"... there rushed to my mind a half-formed thought of joy—of hope... man has many such, which are never completed. I felt that it was of joy—of hope; but I also felt that it had perished in its formation. In vain I struggled to perfect—to regain it. Long suffering had nearly annihilated all my ordinary powers of mind. I was an imbecile—an idiot."

The absurdity of recalling that passage in the circumstances at hand brought a bitter grimace to his blue lips. Yet he felt exactly the way Poe described it: deathly peril; a glimmer of salvation, and frustrating powerlessness to transform the glimmer into a solid beam of light. For a minute—more like eternity—he tried frantically to overcome the paralysis crippling his mind, which resisted his bidding, and to define the idea that refused to be born—an idea that would surely save him, and this only compounded his anguish.

Exactly when did that glimmer startle him like a vision of sudden deliverance, only to dissolve in the night? It couldn't have been very long ago, he felt certain—a few minutes or even seconds. He searched his head to recollect the last few moments—like a writer groping for the right word—when suddenly he remembered the incident that had triggered it. An ordinary, trivial incident, but it held the key to the puzzle on which his life hung. He recalled that the glimmer made him wince just as he started to beat his chest out of desperation.

Yes, that was it. The coincidence had to be significant. His fist striking his chest had touched something, a hard object. Something in his upper left-hand pocket. What could it be? The wheels of his mind turned ever so slowly, but not too slowly for him to find the answer. The object belonged in that pocket. There was no cause for surprise at finding it there. He should have thought of it before he began to pound his chest. It was...

At last the light streamed through. It was the silent whistle he had used to train dolphins and that had turned out to be so effective in communicating with the blue whale. The act of forcing his mind to solve the problem struck him as so significant that it filled him with joy far out of proportion to the trifling value of the discovery. But instinct persuaded him that this whistle was the instrument of his salvation.

He was so convinced of it that, half dead from the cold, he paused a second to still his wildly beating heart, then took the whistle out of his pocket—oh, so carefully! terrified lest it slip out of his numb fingers—removed its waterproof plastic wrapper, placed it in his mouth, and began emitting the vibrations the blue whale had learned to obey.

His instinct had not failed him. So confident of himself was he that it came as no surprise, only as the immense joy of deliverance, when the sea began to boil beneath him and the enormous expanse of the blue whale's back, broad as an island, heaved him above the foaming waters.

10

"**W**E ALL were pretty discouraged by the poor results of our search. We kept it up from a sense of duty, without much hope. Our searchlights couldn't penetrate the fog, and the flares we put up looked like red dots that shed no light. All around us, the dinghies we had lowered were groping blindly through the water. Pitiful results: only one survivor, still alive but in bad shape, and several bodies. Later I realized that a strong current had carried the castaways far beyond where we were looking. I was fretting and fuming and feeling totally helpless on the bridge. Just at that moment, Bjorg, the blue whale appeared.

"A sailor noticed her rubbing up against the hull, as she used to do when she wanted to play. Maybe she'd been waiting there unnoticed for some time. You can imagine how eager we were for fun and games! Anyway, to attract our attention she sprayed the deck by exhaling her moisture-laden breath. Put yourself in my shoes, Bjorg; I was furious, exasperated at her insistent demand for attention when there we were struggling desperately against time. For once the officers and crew shared my annoyance at Auntie Margot. Her behavior appeared inexcusably tactless and I ordered them to send her on her way. One of the sailors was about to do so when he shouted out to me that she wasn't alone and I'd better take a look. I leaned over while he held his flashlight close enough to touch her. I saw what seemed to be a blurred form stretched out on her enormous back, wedged against the dorsal fin. It was you, Bjorg. Can you believe it, Doc? There he lay."

"I have to believe you," said the doctor, "since I'm looking at him now, nearly recovered and back aboard the *Daring*."

"And am I happy to be here, Doc! I thought that never again would I set eyes on this dear ship."

"What do you say to all this, Padre?"

"I'll tell you later, after I hear the rest of Clark's story, if it doesn't tire you, Bjorg."

"I feel strong enough to listen for hours. Please go on, sir."

The former whaler lay on a couch in the lieutenant commander's own cabin. All the beds in sickbay were occupied by survivors of the sunken ship, many of whom had been picked up by the *Daring*, while many more lay in passageways or on the main deck wrapped in whatever coverings could be hastily assembled. The destroyer had been ordered to leave the battle zone and rendezvous with a hospital ship in calmer waters. The doctor and the padre had gone aboard to treat and comfort the many wounded. Having made their rounds, they both ended up at Bjorg's bedside, where Clark was paying a visit.

The former whaler had regained consciousness several hours earlier, and Hodges confirmed the diagnosis of the ship's medical officer: there was no reason to worry about Bjorg's condition; he'd come off with nothing worse than a bad cold, the best medicine for which was a stiff shot of whiskey, even at this hour of the morning. Now that his ship was out of the danger zone after one hellish evening and night, Clark could afford to relax a bit. He had a bottle sent in and they drank to Bjorg's health, while the captain went on with his story of the night's adventure.

"It was you, Bjorg, in a pretty sorry state," he continued. "We couldn't tell if you were dead or alive. We had a hard time tearing you away from that fin you were hanging onto for dear life; your hand wouldn't let it go, even when you were unconscious."

"That's the last thing I remember about being in the water," murmured Bjorg. "I grabbed the base of that fin after flopping onto Auntie Margot's back. I felt as if I were lying on the floor of a lifeboat, and she did her best to steady that blessed platform and keep it above the waves so that I wouldn't slide off."

"Blessed is not too strong a word," the padre interjected.

"She was just as careful when she came up close to

the destroyer," Clark went on. "So we finally managed to pry you loose and the medics looked after you. It seems you had only fainted. You came around pretty fast and the ship's doctor said you were out of danger."

"He has a constitution that thrives on fire and ice," Hodges commented with a shrug.

"Thank you, sir. I'd like to hear more about my rescue later, if you don't mind. But what happened to the whale?"

"The whale? That's the most amazing thing I've ever witnessed, though she's treated us to some pretty unusual stunts. We had hardly relieved her of her passenger than Auntie Margot slipped through our fingers, so to speak, before the crew had a chance to cheer and thank her. She vanished into the night, after sounding, I think, as if she had something far more important on her mind than accepting praise. Vanished? Just temporarily, I mean. I knew she would be back; my intuition told me so. Bjorg, I owe you an apology for arguing with you about that animal's intelligence. I ordered the ship to keep circling the zone we were in so she could find us more easily."

"Did she return?"

"She was back a few minutes later. Once again, as you probably guessed, she was not alone. She had four soldiers on her back whom she probably found huddled together, clinging to some floating scrap of wreckage. Three were still conscious, though near-frozen. They were holding up the fourth, who had blacked out. They too had understood and cooperated with Auntie Margot's rescue efforts; they knew she would get them to safety."

"Incredible behavior for an animal," murmured Hodges, looking at the padre.

"So she delivered the castaways, we hoisted them aboard just as we did you, and off she went again, indefatigable... But you must be getting tired, Bjorg. You need to rest. We'll go now."

"Rest?" grumbled the former whaler, "you think I can sleep? I'd like some more whiskey. You say she went off again?"

"Again and again. Tireless, determined to carry out a mission assigned perhaps by the god of whales, who knows? She kept this up almost all night. She would go off for a few minutes, sometimes a quarter of an hour, sometimes longer, but she never failed to bring back a load of those poor fellows we never were able to find. I couldn't see her until she eased alongside the ship, but I can imagine her slipping silently through this murky sea."

"I can imagine her too, sir," Bjorg muttered pointedly. "I see her gliding through the waves, guided by that infallible, mysterious sense possessed by marine mammals, keener than a pointer's nose, searching relentlessly, just as she scoured the ocean for magnetic mines."

"The only difference being that this time her instinct led her to some wretched human victims of misfortune," Hodges commented.

"Instinct? Come now, Doc! Intelligence—motivation—I've told you over and over."

"Motivation that seems to have been inspired by pure charity," the padre insisted.

"I can't be as certain as you," Hodges grumbled, "but I'm not going to argue the matter. So she made this round trip not once but several times?"

"All night long, Doc, I'm telling you. Until dawn, until..."

"Till she was certain there were no more survivors, that's the truth," Bjorg declared.

"I was watching the whole incredible performance and I believe you're right. Each time she returned to the ship, in order to signal us before we could see her, she practically blew her lungs out."

They would have gone on and on about the whale's epic deeds if Clark hadn't received a phone call from the admiral. After he was gone, the three men fell silent for a long time, lost in the same daydream. Then got up to leave so that Bjorg could rest. Preparations were under way on deck to transfer the wounded to an approaching hospital ship.

"I repeat my question, Padre," Hodges said. "What do you think of all this? You said you'd answer me after hearing the rest of Clark's story."

"'The Spirit breathes where it chooses,'" quoth the padre. "That's what I think."

"What do I hear, Mr. Clark? Your whale has made the front page again?"

"Indeed she has, sir, with a display of heroic dedication that, if she were human, would merit the highest honors."

"Tell me about it—calmly, if you can."

At dawn the high command had inquired into the number of survivors collected by the rescue units. The destroyer *Daring* had retrieved the most by far, around fifty. To Grant, who had called him an hour before, still under the strain of the night's adventure, Clark took pains to elaborate the whale's contribution. His report was so enthusiastic that the astonished chief of staff relayed it word for word to his chief.

The admiral hadn't slept a wink, worrying about the losses in men and material during yesterday's raid, but also comforted somewhat by news of the successful nighttime landing. Nearly all the troops were ashore and heading inland; recapture of the large eastern island was well on its way. Reassured on that score, and puzzled by Grant's report, he took time out to ponder this latest performance of the whale and, even before snatching a few minutes' sleep, insisted on hearing the tale from the lips of its principal witness, LCDR Clark.

Clark obliged by recounting the whole affair, starting with the futile search attempts and the rescue of Bjorg right up to the whale's last appearance, bringing the total number of salvaged souls to fifty-five. When the story ended, after a long thoughtful pause, the admiral spoke gravely.

"I expect that everything you've told me, Mr. Clark, is scrupulously accurate, yes? There's no possiblity that this bloody fog played on your imagination?"

"Upon my word, sir," Clark protested. "Ask any of my officers and crew; ask the fifty-five survivors, beginning with Bjorg, who called to the whale for help."

"I believe you, Mr. Clark," said the admiral pensively. "Not for a minute do I doubt your word, nor do I have to verify it. What we already know about this whale seems to prove that she is no ordinary beast. You call her Auntie Margot, don't you?"

"The sailors christened her that, sir."

"Good. If she distinguishes herself further in one way or another, I want to know about it."

The admiral entered his cabin, lost in thoughts quite unrelated to current operations. After an hour's nap, he returned to his desk and spent the morning issuing orders to various units of the fleet and receiving reports of troop movements that confirmed the success of the landing. Hard as he tried to concentrate on military matters, his mind kept wandering, as if preoccupations of another sort were nagging him. More than once his chief of staff had to repeat questions requiring urgent decisions before he could obtain the admiral's answer.

Just before noon Grant brought him a message from the Admiralty that he must have decoded personally, for it was marked "strictly confidential."

11

THE ADMIRAL had three distinct, pressing considera-
tions on his mind that morning and couldn't decide which
deserved priority: the unpleasant fact of having suffered
losses beyond his expectations; the satisfying achieve-
ment of a successful landing operation despite those losses;
and the remarkable discovery of an animal's courageous
gallantry. Just as he was thinking about all this, his chief
of staff, visibly unnerved by the prospect of braving an
impending storm, came in to deliver a confidential message for him.

"From the Admiralty, sir. They're passing on to you
some remarks from the censor's office concerning mail
sent out earlier by servicemen in the expeditionary force."

"And?"

"Well," Grant continued, his voice dropping, "all
the letters go on at some length about the whale."

"The whale, do they really? And what if they do?"
The admiral's tone boded no good.

"The head of the service saw no reason to censor the letters, since no military secrets were involved, but..."

"That's all we'd need!"

"But he felt he ought to alert the Admiralty to a peculiar, not to say alarming, attitude prevalent among the naval and land forces. With that in mind, the Admiralty in turn suggests that the state of mind reflected in the bulk of the correspondence is not precisely what is expected of..."

The admiral broke into a roar. "Hand me that paper!"

He read the message at a glance; his eyes narrowed, his jaws clenched, his eyebrows closed ranks in battle formation, while the chief of staff wished he could have melted out of sight and cursed his luck for having to deliver such a message at such a moment. Grant expected an explosion, but the admiral snatched at this occasion to perform his own act of heroism by displaying self-control.

"Reply as follows, Mr. Grant," he directed, almost softly. "And for once, I don't want you to alter a single word or comma of my text, even if you feel it doesn't meet the demands of military convention. Write:

"'Thanks for your warning. Peculiar attitude...' That's the word they used, peculiar, isn't it, Mr. Grant?"

"Peculiar, not to say alarming, sir."

"Good. 'Peculiar, not to say alarming attitude' underlined three times, please, 'has indeed infected naval and land forces. Latest victim is myself, fleet admiral of the Falklands expedition. Have pleasure of informing you that Auntie Margot, our whale, will receive citation today on behalf of naval and land forces as follows: Distinguished blue whale...' What's the scientific name they give her, Mr. Grant?"

"*Sibbald's rorqual*, or *Sibbaldus musculus* in Latin, sir," replied the chief of staff without batting an eyelash.

"Perfect. '*Sibbaldus musculus*, known as Auntie Margot, distinguished blue whale, on numerous occasions has rendered incalculable service to the Falkland Islands expedition. In particular, detected and enabled the dismantling of several magnetic mines threatening units of fleet. Also, during the night of'—you fill in the date, precise time, and details, Mr. Grant—'following sinking of a troop transport by enemy aircraft, rushed to scene of diaster, with utter disregard for personal safety, displayed exceptional gallantry and devotion to duty by saving the lives of fifty-five soldiers and sailors and delivering them safely to search ships otherwise unable to locate them.' Are you with me, Mr. Grant?"

"Word for word, sir," replied the chief of staff, writing furiously, having learned from experience that it was useless and even dangerous to offer objections under certain conditions.

"Add this: 'If such display of courageous devotion still strikes you as peculiar for a cetacean, advise you to read Pliny the Elder's *Natural History*, especially the book on dolphins.' Which book, Mr. Grant? I believe there are several."

"There are thirty-seven, sir. I think it's book nine, but I'll check."

In view of the extraordinary magnetism of this cult

of the whale and the admiral's growing interest in it, Grant had felt it his duty to become an expert on marine mammals. Bjorg, who knew not only everything there was to know about cetaceans, but the literature on that subject as well, had agreed to teach him all he could.

"Good idea to check it. And add something else: 'This citation includes the award of a medal for outstanding service that, in recognition of the special character of the recipient, will take the form of a symbolic ceremony, and the decoration will be conferred on the destroyer *Daring,* in whose company the blue whale achieved her noble exploits.' That is all, Mr. Grant. I have nothing more to add for the moment. Did you hear me?"

"Yes, indeed, sir. Allow me to ask if you intend to make this citation official?"

"Do I intend? Dammit, Mr. Grant, the Queen herself couldn't make me change my mind. And after you've sent it to the Admiralty, I want it circulated to the fleet and the army as well, on land, sea, and in the air, and if anyone of any rank has the nerve to find it peculiar, if any officer or deckhand dares to greet this announcement with a grin, not to say the trace of a smirk, I want to hear about it immediately, do you understand, no matter what time of day or night it happens to be, even if there's an air-raid alert, and I will personally discipline the insolent offender, whether he's a commodore or a general. I want that clearly understood as well, Mr. Grant."

"Aye, aye, sir," Grant replied, winding up his notes. "If you'll let me express an opinion, sir, I doubt that such insolence exists in our task force."

"I don't think it does either, but it never hurt anyone to be forewarned."

After a lengthy silence the admiral spoke out resolutely, as if the spawning of his literary effort had eased his soul. "Well, Mr. Grant, don't you agree that this whale is a marvelous creature?"

"'Marvelous' is no exaggeration, sir."

"And that this citation is only a faint token of the gratitude we owe her?"

"A faint token, sir, I agree."

"She's worth her weight in gold, and I am weighing my own words. By the way, who's that Oriental potentate they put on a scale every so often and make him a gift of his own weight in gold?"

"It's the Aga Khan, sir."

"That's what we ought to do with Auntie Margot," declared the admiral, delighted. "How much could that come to, would you say, Mr. Grant?"

"Based on the length of our whale, Bjorg has estimated her weight at about one hundred fifty tons, sir."

"One hundred fifty tons," the admiral mused, totally relaxed now. "She deserves such a reward. Add a postscript to our message to the Admiralty, Mr. Grant, and note that. A hundred fifty tons of gold."

12

AFTER the landing, the recapture of the Falklands proceeded smoothly, as expected. In a perfectly classic maneuver out of the annals of war, British forces traversed Soledad Island along back roads designated by the enemy as unfit for travel, led by Bjorg and other native-born guides who knew those routes intimately. Restored to health forty-eight hours after his forced bath, the former whaler had insisted on carrying out his scouting job. The Argentineans were poorly trained and equipped, unused to the severe cold, and commanded by inept generals; day by day their resistance crumbled. Port Darwin collapsed within twenty-four hours. Gurkha reinforcements arrived to ensure the victory. The capital, Port Stanley, was encircled and fell, the last bastion, where enemy troops had managed to cut themselves off. Their surrender presaged the close of a one-sided struggle on terra firma.

Bombs went on falling and caused further damage to the fleet, but after several airfields were seized and converted by the British into landing bases for their own planes, the raids decreased, proved less effective, and finally ceased altogether following Port Stanley's capture.

It was a de facto truce, leading up to the formal armistice. The admiral allowed modest celebrations aboard all ships. He himself hosted a gathering for some of the officers who had distinguished themselves during the fighting, but cautioned them not to relax their vigilance. He was afraid the gallant Argentine pilots might attempt some desperate last-minute foray, in keeping with their past record—perhaps a suicide mission for honor's sake, to inflict a parting blow at the victors.

The admiral was right to be wary, but wrong to assess the only real threat as airborne. His mistake was understandable since, from the opening of hostilities, the heaviest destruction had fallen from the skies, so it made sense to regard the air force as the one serious menace. Fighting on land had been merely sporadic. As for the Argentine navy, aside from a submarine near the coast of South Georgia that had yielded without firing a shot, not a single antiquated vessel from its mothball fleet had dared to challenge the mighty British armada.

Yet it was one of these, a submarine, small and shopworn, but armed with torpedoes, that set out to cast an avenging blow at the intruders. Having escaped detection, under cover of darkness (which stretched far into the morning), it had managed to skirt the Falklands and approach the fleet. Lurking on the bottom of the sea, with motors silenced, it sat waiting for big game. Luck was on its side. British ships cruising lazily in that area chanced to draw near the hidden hunter.

Several escort vessels—destroyers, frigates, and corvettes—passed over the little submarine. The hydrophones detected no engine noises. The asdics revealed nothing suspicious among all the echoes bouncing off wreckage that littered the ocean floor around the Falklands, some of it recently deposited by sunken warships and planes, most of it from the more than one hundred thirty shipwrecks recorded over the centuries in those storm-ridden waters off beaconless shores.

The little submarine let the escort vessels pass. It was not planning to waste its precious ammunition on small fry. A suicide mission has to pay off. It sat waiting for the admiral's flagship, the aircraft carrier every other ship was bound to protect. Wiping out a target of such grand scale was one way to erase the memory of a humiliating defeat and to avenge the Argentineans who had perished in the Falklands.

Only after it sighted the giant's distant shadow did the submarine gear up and launch the devices it carried: three operable torpedoes, the others having proved defective.

The wake of the first two was spotted by a corvette: sounding the alarm, she rushed to where a bubbly froth marked the source. The carrier's skipper had time to turn sharply and get out of the way. A classic maneuver the little submarine had gambled on. The change of direction shifted the admiral's ship around, placing its side squarely in the path of the third torpedo, which advanced undetected below the surface. But even detection would not have helped at this stage, for the device, though slow-moving, was target-seeking—electronically designed to home in on an object no matter what the object did to avoid it.

Having accomplished its self-chosen mission, the little submarine prepared to meet the same fate as the carrier's and yielded to depth charges flung out by the pursuing corvette. It seemed that nothing could save the flagship, whose serpentine maneuvers to escape the first torpedoes simply placed it at the mercy of the third.

At this moment a new trail suddenly began to etch itself on the waters of the Falklands. The blue whale was watching. The blue whale had been content to hear the last of the roaring guns and bursting bombs convulsing her universe. Relieved of the stress imposed by a perpetual state of alarm, Auntie Margot had resumed her tranquil meanderings on the ocean's face, interspersed with a shallow dive or two. But Auntie Margot kept a sharp ear out for trouble. Unlike the admiral's guests, who were busy congratulating one another, she saw no cause for celebrating a victory whose significance escaped her. Auntie Margot never slept and never relaxed her vigil, while her adopters grew dull-eyed toasting their triumph.

The release of the first torpedoes had revived her fears and left her with the impression that the truce was precarious and the whole affair not truly resolved. She swam closer, guided by the new sound of a motorized device altogether different from the familiar noise of ships' motors. The strange buzz, like the drone of hostile aircraft during the past few days, could only mean danger. This sense of menace was further confirmed by the wake of one of the torpedoes that passed close to her. Any creature capable of carving such a path through the water was up to no good. Tempted to give chase, she decided against it, for the enemy—and what else could it be?—swam faster than she could. At least thirty knots, she estimated, against her own best speed of only twenty. No point wearing herself out in a race she could never win. Anyway, another threat loomed; she perceived its vibrations.

This one she could handle. She had spotted it in time to intercept it if she made a right-angle turn. Undulating her immense body to gain all possible speed—for there wasn't a minute to lose—the blue whale charged at the foe.

Their paths converged when the mechanism was scarcely a hundred yards from the carrier. The inevitable, dreadful explosion shook the ship and sent debris flying against the hull. A colossal column of water swept skyward, part of which hit the deck, but there was no damage to report.

When the waves subsided, from the carrier's streaming deck the admiral and his guests looked out on a mangled carcass bobbing on the waves, surrounded by an enormous oil stain splotched with blood, which kept spreading, reaching out to mingle with another oil spill, witness to the final, glorious passage of the little submarine.

13

THIS final act of the blue whale stirred the hearts of the sailors who witnessed it, though they were not strangers to the tragedies of war. It drew passionate comments from the admiral's guests on the flight deck. The admiral himself set the mood of mourning by doffing his cap and observing a minute's silence. At the close of this ultimate homage, he announced:

"An act of heroism that rarely occurs in the human community, gentlemen, but never have I heard of such self-sacrifice in the animal kingdom."

The padre gave his blessing. He repeated a favorite quotation of his that often had crept into his conversations with Hodges: "'The Spirit breathes where it chooses'; the Bible tells us this is so, even in the creature world where we least expect to find it."

Lieutenant Commander Clark, one of the guests,

said nothing. He knew he would break down and cry if he opened his mouth.

Dr. Hodges was as deeply moved as the others, but recovered his composure faster. He was thinking aloud.

"Strange," he murmured. "Spirit, you call it, Padre? I shan't argue with you, but it would take thousands of observations to reach any conclusion. Some competent scientists might take a very different view. Perhaps we're simply dealing with a physical reflex."

"Physical reflex!" the padre protested in concert with other officers, while the admiral frowned ominously.

"I'm simply presenting certain arguments favored by some of my colleagues for whom animal behavior is merely instinctual and never the product of reason. They would assure you that in every respect a killer whale resembles an elongated torpedo gliding through the water. The hatred these whales feel for the killers, their ancestral foe, is imprinted on each of the millions of cells that make up their monstrous bodies and is the legacy of centuries of experience. So if a killer is seen alone, isolated from the pack in which it always hunts, the whale needs no second invitation to pursue and crush it under the weight of its hundred and fifty tons."

"I don't go for that theory," Clark objected.

"Nor I," echoed the padre.

"I can't stand it," the admiral murmured.

"I'm not trying to ram it down your throats, you know, so let me suggest another, since I don't feel qualified to take a stand. Other equally competent scientists who have followed the train of events since the whale first appeared could well maintain that this is a case of accelerated evolution. First, pure instinct, which made her approach your ship, Clark, after you saved her life; the memory of that peril associated with the ship's proximity gave her a sense of security. Next, budding thought, after more or less random efforts, in the course of which she found that certain things she did removed obstacles in her path. Remember her pensive look before she decided to approach the starboard side. Spiritual development, Padre, slow to emerge, culminating in a sense of gratitude after we rid her of those parasites; then devotion to her duty, as she understood it, of rescuing drowning creatures to whom she felt deeply obligated. And, finally, today, some would say that what she did reflected a decision to sacrifice herself."

"The highest manifestation of the spirit," the padre nodded approvingly.

"I subscribe to that theory," the admiral concluded.

When the war in the Falklands ended, there was peace again in that doorway to Antarctica, domain of the seal, the penguin, and a few blue whales that came back to haunt those waters despite the recurring threat of relentless harpooners.

The British fleet resumed its regular maneuvers in familiar seas. Bjorg is still trying to improve communications with his dolphins. The Gurkhas rejoined their outfits and, at the close of military service, some returned to their mountain homelands to help erect a temple in honor of the god Vishnu the Preserver, incarnated for his tenth and final avatar in the form of an azure-blue whale shimmering with gold. Ever-growing throngs of worshippers come there to pray and offer gifts.

Hodges has carried on interminable discussions with his medical colleagues concerning the behavior of this animal from the standpoint of comparative psychology. The padre, with permission from church officials, held a memorial service for the blue whale. Clark saw to it that the medal bestowed on Auntie Margot was hung in the place of honor on the bridge of the *Daring*. The admiral is moving heaven and earth to have her awarded the most coveted decoration of all, the Victoria Cross, posthumously. The Duke of Edinburgh has heard all about the affair and is supporting the admiral's application. Joan shed a tear when she read the letters about Auntie Margot's final exploit.

After looking in at home, all the sailors of the destroyer *Daring* and the carrier went into mourning.